SILT

GOOD DIRT

Volume I

SILT

GOOD DIRT

Volume I

The River Bottom Writers

Original Photography by Ken Orich.

Watson, Bianca
Silt: Good Dirt Volume I / Bianca Watson.–1st ed.

Summary: A captivating collection of short stories and poems from the members of The River Bottom Writers, a group of creative minds based in Southern Alberta. The following selections are works shared by members at group gatherings and parties over the six years they have been together. Organized by season, these stories and poems range from insightful and heartfelt to chilling, dramatic, and outright hilarious. The River Bottom Writers invite you to sample an anthology of some of their favourite pieces.

ISBN 978-0-9948513-7-6 (Softcover : alk, paper) / 978-0-9948513-8-3 (e-book)
[1. Fiction. 2. Anthologies (multiple authors)] I. Title.

Designed by David and Bianca Watson | Printed in Canada | First Edition

10 9 8 7 6 5 4 3 2 1

CONTENTS

AUTUMN: HAUNTING AND HARVEST

WINTER: HOLIDAYS AND HIBERNATION

"The scariest moment is always just before you start."

-Stephen King

Introduction

The River Bottom Writers was created in 2012, a dynamic group of like-minded individuals, joined together by their love of writing and dreams of becoming authors.

Led by Leslie Johnson, this Southern Alberta based group has grown from a small, hopeful gathering to a vibrant, supportive community of writers who now meet at the local college to write, give feedback, present on writing tips and keep their vision going strong.

This book is a collection of short stories and poems from the creative minds of our members. The following selections are works shared at group gatherings and parties over the six years the group has been together.

Organized by season, these works range from insightful and heartfelt to chilling, dramatic, and outright hilarious.

We hope you enjoy this anthology of some of our favourite pieces.

SPRING

Cultivation and Celebration

A SIXTH SENSE

By Leslie Johnson

THE AIR AROUND the carnival was electric with teenage energy. Hundreds of young people bounced around from game to game, tossing rings or bowling bottles for small prizes. Laughter filled the air, eventually reaching me inside my quiet tent.

The final hour of the free carnival was winding down. I wondered how many more fortunes I would have to tell before I could breathe a sigh of relief and remove the scarf I had wound around my head. My next client stepped through the curtain and sat down.

The young girl across from me was like every other girl who had come in before her. They blended in my memory as a sea of uniform faces, each one slightly curious and a little afraid. I reached across the wooden table that separated us. Without a word, she placed her left hand in mine and I tugged it closer. Looking at the road map of lines on her slightly moist palm, I furrowed my brow in concentration. What did this hand tell me about the girl sitting across from me? I waited a good minute, turning her hand this way and that to get a better look. Then I began.

Tracing my finger along her palm, I said. "You have a long life line. A few bumpy years later in life. See here where there are crosses on the line?"

She nodded, looking at me in anticipation.

"It's nothing serious. Those lines aren't long, can you see?" She pulled her hand back to see more clearly. When she relaxed again, I twisted it slightly to get a better look. "Your love line is rocky." This time I ran my finger-nail along the shorter line that ran below her pinkie and scooped up toward her index finger. "You will have many loves for the next few years but then, see here…"

She leaned forward to see where I was pointing. "This line here is where you cross paths with your soul-mate. And the rest will be history. Your love line is mostly smooth after that."

"You see all that in my hand?" she asked, her eyes wide.

"That and more. Your hand tells a story all the way to grandchildren and beyond. And it changes as you go forward. You will be happy and content with your life."

She sat for a moment, perhaps wondering what to say. Then she stood up. "Thank you. I can't wait to see what life brings."

I nodded.

Pulling back the curtain, she left. A few seconds later, a petite brunette peeked through the opening. "Is it my turn now?"

I tilted my head and waved my hand toward the chair. "Please, take a seat."

She slipped forward and sat gingerly on the edge of the chair. I studied her. Wispy tendrils of dark hair framed a pair of soft brown eyes. The cheeks of her heart shaped face bore the slightly rosy tone of someone enjoying the adventures of the carnival. She seemed familiar somehow, yet I couldn't remember her name.

"Where's your crystal ball?" she asked looking around. I smiled.

"I am a palm reader. I can tell you all you need to know by looking at your hand."

Without preamble, she stuck her hand across at me. I paused for half beat debating whether to ask her for her other hand, just to be contrary. Instead, I smiled and gently took her offered hand, turning her palm toward me. Looking at it, my heart dropped. Her life line was short, her love line practically non-existent.

As I did with every person that came in, I studied her hand silently, trying to gather my thoughts. What would I say to this slip of a girl? I really didn't know how to read palms, I was playing a game. I stuffed back the thoughts that had popped into my head and began to conjure a brighter future.

I looked up into her brown eyes and smiled. "I see you taking a trip. A long trip. Perhaps a honeymoon with your true love: dark haired, tall and very handsome. He will bring you joy and happiness for the rest of your days."

"Really?"

"Without question. You are blessed." I turned her hand toward the light but no words came to me. I was out of my depth. I asked for her other hand.

The lines on this hand were similar. What did it matter, I said to myself. Just tell her anything. Looking up, I traced my finger along her right palm.

"I see a few babies in your future. There are at least two, but the line isn't complete. There may be more."

She stood up abruptly, pulling her hand from me. "Thank you!" Turning on her heel she prepared to leave. Before she slipped through the curtain, she paused and looked back at me. "Thank you, really." Then, she was gone.

I sat back, feeling suddenly older than my seven-teen years. It was only make-believe this sixth sense I was pretending to have. But somehow I knew what I had seen on her left palm was true. She didn't have long to live.

The announcement came for the group to re-assemble in the gym. I pulled off my scarf, thankful this part of the night was over. Playing a palm reader and having to say something bright and new to each person was harder than I imagined when I volunteered. I had no experience to draw from. I based this character on a gypsy woman I'd seen on an episode of Get Smart. I'd never been to a psychic or a medium, but it sounded like more fun than pitching balls or tossing rings.

The curtain was pulled back and Grant Fletcher stepped into the room. "You did great. Did you have fun?"

I smiled. Grant was part of the organization running this week long festival. He and I had a history, we'd met on several occasions and I liked him. He sat down opposite me.

"Do you want your palm read?" I asked, hoping he would say no.

Laughing, he shook his head. "No, thanks." Then he became serious. "I've been sitting out there for a while. I heard what you said to Debbie. That was nice."

Debbie? Which one was Debbie? I'd met a hundred kids this week, probably more than one Debbie. In the two hours I'd been the palm reader this night, I'd spoken to only one young man and twenty some girls.

Which one was Debbie?

Then it clicked.

Debbie - the little dark haired pixie girl with the short life line. "Thank you, but it was nothing special."

"It was special. She has leukemia. She was in remission, but…" His words faded, a cloud dropping over his face. "Please don't say anything. No one is supposed to know."

But I did know - the short line of her life. It was clear now. My stomach flipped.

"What you said to that girl, was precious. You really are something special, Tracy." Grant stood up, leaned over the table and kissed me full on the mouth.

Sparks exploded around my head, or maybe they were stars. I'd never been kissed like that in my life. It threw my senses into overdrive and they sped around in every direction until my head began to swim. Stepping back, he offered me his hand. "Let's go. I think this is our dance."

It was then the music reached my ears. I hadn't heard it start. I stood up on wobbly legs and took his hand. Together we crossed the auditorium to the gym where he swirled me into his arms and onto the floor. When the dance ended, Jack, a boy from my hometown appeared at my elbow.

Grant released me to take a spin around the floor with Jack. I caught one last glimpse of him at the edge of the crowd before I was turned around. When I tried to find him later, he was gone. With a sigh, I knew that whatever was there was gone too. Call it my sixth sense rising anew.

I never saw Grant Fletcher again, but that night swims through my memory often. He gave me something special - a sense of self - an awareness of my value as a woman and the thrill of being sought out. Although I won't say he was my first love, he certainly was my first kiss.

MARCH IS A FICKLE MISTRESS

By Ken Orich

March is a fickle Mistress.
She can come in gentle as a lamb and roar out like a lion
or Roar in like a lion and leave like a lamb.
March is confusing and hard to describe;
so, some sage grandmother explained how March works.

March teases us with melting snow, warm days and running water, sunshine and blue skies, a hint of green, a Robin's song.
About the time we are switching to sandals, shorts and tank tops, she slams us with howling north winds, driven snow, frigid gray skies, freezing cold and Winter's foggy breath.
March is a fickle Mistress; she has no love for you or me.

But wait, hold on. Look carefully and you will see,
the march towards spring has not come to a grinding halt.
Tulips are poking their way towards Spring.
Just because you don't see blossoms,
doesn't mean the world is not in bloom.
March is the beginning; look for other blossoms, pussy willows perhaps.

Have you noticed the iridescent green sheen of a Mallard's head?
Or the shine of red on a Redhead?
Did you notice that butterfly skipping by, on its way to who knows where?
Have you wakened to the "cheer up, cheer up" of a Robin yet?
Have you looked up when honking geese flew overhead?
Were they Snow Geese or did you not care?

Did you notice the Cottonwood buds have swollen in pregnant expectation of birthing leaves?
Have you heard the cry of a hawk, but all you could see was a Starling?
Did you notice the shimmering brilliance of its blue-black

feathers, spiked by a corn-yellow bill?
Have you seen a flash of Mountain Bluebird blue as you were driving along?
If you've seen it once, you will never forget it.

Have you heard a Meadowlark sing to the morning sun?
Not for you or me, but to tell the world it is alive, and all is well.
Its breast reminds me of a yellow blossom in spring and things to come.
Have you seen the scarlet epaulets of a blackbird flashing in the sun?
Have you noticed a fly's bright green eyes or a Lady Bug's red dress with black polka dots?

Did you see the hoar frost in the grass;
or the diamond dust on a spider web?
Have you run your fingers over a soft pussy willow,
or tickled your face with it?
Have you seen a sunset reflected in an icicle?
Did you notice the white, cotton ball clouds skipping across the sky
and know they promised fair weather?

Has the hoot-hoot hoooot of an Owl
caused you to listen more carefully?

So, put away your cell phones.
Turn off your computer.
Kick your kids off their video games.
Send them outside.
Run as fast as you can from Facebook and Twitter.

The world is in bloom,
Mother Nature makes sure of it.
The blossoms are there to find.
Don't let March discourage you.
After all, she is a fickle Mistress.

THE CHANGING WORLD

By Bryan L. Beerling

AFTER GRABBING HIS jacket, Les slipped out of his smock and hung it on the hook. The buzzer ending the last shift at Imperial Optical for the week still sounded as he passed some of his fellow workers.

"Coming to the dance hall tonight?" Clyde called out. Les wanted to ignore the question but being the new boss, he did not want to alienate the staff. He turned half-way around looking back at his co-workers.

"Nah," he said, "after a week's work my chair and the radio sound like a better place for me tonight. Maybe tomorrow."

"Okay," John said, "but I think Marjorie will be there tonight and she is a real looker."

Les had heard about Marjorie, the best looking

girl at the dance hall, but she was not there to dance. She was a volunteer serving drinks and snacks, raising money for the Canadian Red Cross. Many guys had tried to get her on the dance floor but none had succeeded. Even the promise of donations could not sway her.

"What's the use?" Les asked. "According to you she doesn't dance and only wants the donations."

The co-workers leaving work with him laughed as they crossed the empty parking lot.

Just like the city of Saskatoon where Les had come from, the city of Winnipeg had lots of women. Most men left behind were military rejects for one reason or another, many incapable of meeting the strict physical requirements.

Les, local manager at the optical manufacturing company made eyeglass lenses as well as lenses for telescopes and binoculars. He was rejected by the army because his job as a civilian was deemed to be more important than what he could likely contribute as a soldier. He was told that if he quit his job and enlisted, he would likely never see action and would be stuck at a home base for the duration of the war. Desiring to contribute, he kept his job and served however he could.

The workers parted, some walking, some standing at the nearby bus stop. Cars were scarce and costly. War-time rationing made fuel prices soar.

Les crossed the street in the middle of the block. With the lack of cars on the street jaywalking meant no peril. A three story building directly across the street from the office housed his apartment. One room above an abandoned store held his worldly belongings, three sets of clothes, two pairs of shoes, a bed, chair and radio. Except for his treasured record player and a vast collection of records, 33s and 78s, the few shelves remained empty.

Music ranged from country, folk and opera to musicals. People who knew him often teased Les about the money he spent on the records. He knew every word to every song and could sing them better than what you could hear on the scratchy records.

Some people even thought he should turn in his work smock for a harmonica and entertain the troops overseas. The harmonica was the only musical instrument he could play but he was the best anyone ever heard. Only his singing topped that. He didn't think he was that good but enjoyed singing and playing the harmonica.

Les looked out the window. The once manicured

boulevards were now little more than dirt patches. Flower beds were bare. Trees were dying from lack of water. It hurt Les to see that. His father had been a gardener in England and taught him how to care for every living thing as long as it didn't bite back. He would take care of them himself if he knew where the equipment was or how to turn on the city water taps.

He flicked on the radio. There was little choice of radio stations. Only three if you adjusted the antennae for each, and all on the AM dial. FM was unheard of. The static tonight muffled what was being said even after adjusting the antennae. He flicked it off hoping it would be better later in the evening. Les looked through his record collection but couldn't decide what he felt like listening to.

He put his ear up to the wall, listening for his neighbour. He couldn't hear any sound so decided it safe to play his harmonica. His neighbour often objected to the 'racket' of the tin and wooden instrument. He tried a couple of songs but nothing seemed to please him.

His stomach growled.

He hadn't eaten since breakfast. He always worked through his lunch break, trying to show his staff how hard he worked. In the cupboards all he could find was a can of Spam. He looked in the breadbox. A sandwich did not excite him. He closed the cupboard.

Then he thought, 'for a small donation I could get coffee and snacks at the dance hall.'

He checked his pocket: three dollars in change and a one dollar bill. That would be enough. Les walked the three blocks to the dance hall. It was actually just a large room above an abandoned gasoline station. A four member band, all volunteers, were setting up on the stage. Three of his staff, Syd, Ken and Fred sat at a large table along the far wall, each cradling a soda pop bottle.

He asked about the food and learned it would be an hour before things got in motion. His staff were just there to make sure they got a table. Friday night, dancers always packed the hall. It was a place where, for a few hours, people could forget about the happenings in Europe.

Les sat with his staff talking about the good times when it seemed the world was in bloom and nothing could spoil it.

World War One was the war to end all wars. So-called experts in their field were certain there would never be another world dictator. Adolph Hitler was just some loudmouth German that never had enough support to start a back alley fight. As they predicted his demise Hitler gained strength through alliances with other European leaders only to break all promises and sweep most of Europe.

Les relished the years in between the wars. Streets flourished with trees and flower boxes. Instead of gathering at dance halls, city parks were the gathering points where parents spread out blankets and watched their children mix with others playing Red Rover, Kick the Can and Hide and Seek. Parents knew the usual "Already?" or "Do we have to?" followed when the children were called home.

A woman appeared in front of Les and his workers carrying snacks. Coca-cola could be bought at the service counter. Les tossed some of his change in the metal soup can on her tray. The label had been replaced with a handmade one: DONATIONS.

Les pulled open the small packet of mixed nuts she'd given him and watched her walk away. To him, she looked good coming or going. She was not a runway model but she was a looker.

Les leaned over towards Clyde and said, "I'm going to marry that girl."

Eldon heard him and burst out laughing. "That's Marjorie," he managed to say between chortles. "She isn't interested in any local men. She's waiting for the soldiers to return after the war. The war won't last long."

"I'm going to marry that girl," Les repeated and got up from his chair. He had to wend his way through the gathered maze of people to find her. His staff jabbed at each other, laughing and joking, certain Les would come back to the table alone. Clyde choked on his soda as he spotted Les and Marjorie arm in arm on the dance floor.

* * *

More than two decades later Les and Marjorie sat on the front porch of their home in Lethbridge. The war was a distant memory despite lasting four more years.

Their two children were grown and on their own. Their daughter and husband lived half a block away expecting their first grandchild. In those days you found out what sex it was when the doctor held it in his hands.

Their son was in Kingston, Ontario in basic training. They were happy it was peace time and he would not be going to war.

Kitty-corner from their house they could hear the neighborhood children playing in Kintown Park. Their adopted son's voice was easily picked out above the others'. "Red Rover, Red Rover," he called out, "We call Laura over."

Neighbors across the street on either side and down the block were now gathering on their porches in the cooler air of the evening. Houses were still too hot these summer days and only those people living along Henderson Lake could afford air-conditioning.

One block of five Eaton Catalogue houses faced the playground. Those five houses at one time housed twenty-seven of the neighborhood children. Of course that was not hard to understand when you knew nineteen lived in two houses.

When most of the neighbors had gathered, Les reached out and held Marjorie's hand. He started to sing and she sang along. They didn't need music. Neighbours clapped after every song. Marjorie was famous locally for her rendition of Vera Lynn's The Anniversary Waltz but she rarely sang it. It reminded her of the war.

Les was better known for his solo parts with the

Gyro Club choir that often performed at Southminster Church. Coincidently, his most requested song was The Anniversary Song by Andy Williams.

He had also become a hard working volunteer for the Lethbridge Curling Club. Both he and Marjorie also worked hard with the Lethbridge Figure Skating Club. Their greatest pride was their daughter performing as Cinderella a few years ago in the figure skating annual performance. Marjorie had hand-sewn most of the costumes and Les served as chairman of the club.

Their son also excelled at figure skating but when he entered high school, badgering and scoffing by the other boys made him quit.

As daylight faded one child could be heard calling out in the dark, "Eight, nine, ten... Ready or not, here I come." Bushes would move as children hid behind them. Tree branches dipped as older children climbed up the trunk. One or two older pairs of boys and girls could be seen scampering across the street behind houses 'to talk.' Soon rapid footsteps across the paved walkway would sound out and someone would call out, "Home free."

The neighbors knew when Les and Marjorie started singing, "Irene good night, Irene good night. Goodnight Irene, goodnight Irene. I'll see you in my dreams."

It was the last song of the evening and the adults started moving inside, the houses now cooled.

Children also knew it was time to head home. The older ones often took their parents' places on the porch to talk about the upcoming football game with the LCI Rams against those north-siders, the Winston Churchill Bulldogs or their dreaded enemies, the Raymond Comets.

Yes, Les thought, as he watched Bryan scamper across the road from the park to that neighbor's house with the cute blonde girl, 'the world was in bloom.'

THE WORLD WAS IN BLOOM
(And Not In Bloom)
By Vanessa Rieswyk

The world is sad
In winter
And fall
It looks dead

The flowers
The trees
The ground
Don't have colours
They aren't in bloom
White is on everything

People and animals are sad
It is cold

Some animals sleep
In winter
And fall

The world isn't in bloom
In winter
And in fall

There isn't a lot of food
For animals
Because the world
Is not in bloom

When spring
And summer come
The world is in bloom

The flowers
And the trees
Are in bloom
And the ground
Is warmer

People

And animals are happy

Because it's sunny

And warm

The animals

That were sleeping

In the fall

And winter

Are awake

Because it's summer

And spring

In summer

And spring

There is a lot of food

For everyone

Because the world is in bloom

Also there are a lot

Of baby animals

In spring

And summer

But not in winter

Or fall

Because it's cold

In fall

And winter

It's warmer in summer

And spring

And the world

Is in bloom

REMEMBER WHEN

By Bianca Rowena

"REMEMBER WHEN YOU buried your cat in the back yard?" Michael says.

"Yeah and we had that funeral?" I smile. The sun rays peeking between the tree branches warm my face. There's no roof on my tree house, or walls, or a door. So I guess it isn't really a tree house, more like wooden planks set together. Someone had started building a tree house, but never finished it.

I glance over at the house we've just moved into. It's the same as this tree house, broken down and left behind. Part of the roof droops down, like the house is sad.

"I never told you this," Michael says. I turn my head to look at him. His blond hair hangs into his eyes, hiding their usual sparkle.

"Never told me what?" I ask.

"My dog dug up your cat's remains and chewed them."

"He did not!" I smack Michael's shoulder and he draws back. I've never had a cat, but Michael's story makes me almost believe I did.

"Remember when your great grandma's false teeth fell out at that family barbecue at your house last summer?" I ask, enjoying our game.

Michael nods and my heart swells with gratitude. He came up with the 'Remember When' game, just for me. Since I'm the new kid in town, again, I have no childhood memories to share with anyone around here. The only person I know in this town is my dad, because he came with me.

My second week here, I was sitting at a lunch table full of girls in the cafeteria, when the girls kept bringing up stuff that had happened. 'Remember when Annika did this and that?' 'Remember when Jordon said that?'

I couldn't join in the conversation. The whole thing was making me depressed. I left the table and went to walk around the halls. That's were I ran into Michael, sitting on a bench by the large trophy case, earphones in.

I sat down beside him and he took out an ear bud and asked me why I looked so sad. I wasn't used to people at school starting a conversation with me, a stranger, which is what I always am in schools. I was honest with him and told him about how I have no 'remember when's' with friends, because my dad and I move around so much.

He seemed to find that fascinating and he came up with the Remember When Game. It was easy for him, being a natural story teller. I've stayed up many nights reading and re-reading some of his short stories.

"Yes," he says now. "I remember that. Your little sister yelled out 'Michael's great grandma has Leprosy!'"

I laugh. Michael's imagination is so random. I don't have a little sister but he knows I've always wanted one.

"Yes," I say, "and my mom said, 'Leprosy was only a thing back in Jesus' time.'"

"Which isn't true," Michael adds. "Then your sister said, 'Michael's great grandma lived in Jesus' time!'"

We both laugh and Michael rolls across the tree

house floor, almost tumbling off the platform. I scream and grab the back of his t-shirt.

"It's okay," he laughs. "I'm not going to fall. I was just pretending."

"Not funny!" My heart pounds. "You could have died."

Michael laughs even harder. "I'd break an arm or something, but I wouldn't die."

Just then his cell phone vibrates, startling him and he almost does fall off the side. He pulls it out of his pocket and looks at the screen. His smile quickly turns into a frown.

"It's my dad," he says, answering the call. "Hello? No. I'm with her right now." He glances at me briefly, then turns his back to me. "Yes. Okay."

That's the whole conversation.

When Michael turns back around there's no trace of the laughter left on his face from moments ago.

"I gotta go," he says.

I get up. "Right now?"

Michael steps off the side of the platform and jumps.

My heart leaps and I shut my eyes, catching my

breath. I hear the elastics of the trampoline below, then open my eyes again. Michael does an impressive flip into the air and lands on his knees on the trampoline.

Did he do that to prove something? He knows I hate it when he jumps onto the trampoline from this high. And I know he hates it when I tell him that I hate it.

I scramble down the splintering wooden ladder, nailed to the tree trunk, and jump into the tall grass.

"Wait!" I yell. "Maybe my dad can call your dad and ask if you can stay for lunch."

"No," Michael says.

"What's your dad's number?"

Michael doesn't reply so I grab his phone.

"Don't!" Michael snatches it back. "If you ever call my parents I'll never talk to you again."

I freeze in place.

Michael walks away. He scales the back gate in one impressive leap, landing on the other side.

Then, he's gone.

The Earth begins to quake. Or my legs do. I lower myself into the tall grass, which rises up on either side of me. There are no sounds, this low to the ground, only smells; the fresh smells of spring.

I always wished we could move to a place with a tree house and a big back yard. I look up at the planks in the tree. It's not really a tree house. When I first saw it I thought my dreams were coming true. But they weren't. I'd give them all up just to hear the sound of Michael's footsteps on the other side of the back gate, returning to say he's not mad and that I'll fit in here, and his parents don't hate me.

A lonely lady bug climbs up a thick blade of grass, catching my attention. It's brilliantly red amidst all the new green. I put out my finger and let it climb onto my hand.

"Hello," I say. I've done this before, made friends with lady bugs. But no matter how much you care for them, they always die or escape the jar in the end. You can't force a lady bug to be your friend, or even to stay alive for you.

The tiny, red bug crawls across my dark skin. I turn my palm up to let it move towards the center of my hand. This one will fly away too, and leave me, if I don't do something. I know what I will do. At least then it will be decision and I won't be abandoned.

Before I can close my hand around it to crush it,

the lady bug flies away, over the back gate, the same way Michael did.

BUSINESS AS USUAL

By Leslie Johnson

IT WAS LONG past Groundhog Day, when the world, in all its glory, was in bloom. I was riding an emotional rollercoaster and at that moment, I was madder than a wet hen.

I caught the apple of my eye with his hand in the cookie jar. He has a face only a mother could love and it caught me off guard – again. Thankfully he wasn't caught with his pants down. That would be a sight for sore eyes. He started giving me the old cock and bull story. How many times had I asked him to change his tune?

"All work and no play makes Jack a dull boy!" Jack started.

I cut him off at the pass. "An idle mind is the devil's playground, you imbecile. And the early bird gets the worm."

"Another day and another dollar is another nail in my coffin."

"Are you a man or a mouse?"

As luck would have it, we were interrupted. It was his mother who was built like a brick shithouse. As always, she was as welcome as a skunk at a lawn party. She batted her baby blues and said, "Can't you see his back is against the wall. Give him a break, for crying out loud. He's a babe in the woods not bad to the bone. Don't send him back to the salt mines." She turned her attention to me. "I see you're having a bad hair day."

If she was trying to get a rise out of me, she was barking up the wrong tree. Even though it was not the eleventh hour, I could tell she was bombed - plastered - out of her gourd, three sheets to the wind. "Get a life," I sneered. "I believe in calling a spade a spade. Your son sits around like a bump on the log most days. If I didn't have a bun in the oven he wouldn't need to burn the candle at both ends. But I do, so there is no time like the present."

"Can it," my husband interrupted. "Cry me a river, Jill. You can't get blood from a stone if you catch my drift."

His mother patted his cheek, "You're a chip off the old block."

"As usual, it's pretty cut and dried, isn't it?" I snapped. "That makes me chief cook and bottle washer."

"Now cut that out!" my father-in-law, a few fries short of a happy meal, shouted. "If you want him to do something, dangle a carrot in front of him. Don't chew him out."

I reached the end of the rope. "Shut up! You all drive me crazy! And you," I said pointing at Jack. "Are a thorn in my side. A good man is hard to find."

"Now dear," my father-in-law interjected, "seriously, it's really as easy as pie." He had such a heart of gold and was firing on all cylinders. We were heading for a Mexican standoff. I needed to cut the brough-ha-ha off at the pass.

"I think we got off on the wrong foot here," I said. It was a good rule of thumb to give a glimmer of hope to a half-baked idea. I was beginning to think I should cut bait and move on to greener pastures despite the creature growing like a weed in my belly. I had it up to here with this Jack of all trades and master of none.

Except I knew which side my bread was buttered on! I lived in the land of milk and honey.

A leopard cannot change his spots. It was time to let bygones be bygones and let sleeping dogs lie. My husband can be like a bull in a china shop but love is blind. There is more to him than meets the eye. And though we are as different as night and day - as chalk and cheese - he is my knight in shining armour. I guess there is no accounting for taste. Besides, there is no place like home. I decided to take another stab at it.

"I'm not asking you to work your fingers to the bone," I ventured. I had to play my cards right.

Jack replied, "There's more than one way to skin a cat."

"True, but there's something fishy about that." I knew I was going to have to call off the dogs.

"You're tugging at my heartstrings, babe. I'm gonna turn on a dime here."

"Are you yanking my chain? Don't go overboard."

Cool as a cucumber, he smiled. "Nope. I'm going out with a bang - you can take that to the bank!"

You could have knocked me over with a feather. He was going to do what it took to finish the baby's room before I popped. "Don't paint yourself in a corner!" I called after him feeling proud as a peacock.

"The best laid plans of mice and men, eh?" my mother-in-law said. "We're a winning combination, you and I. We've got him working like a dog."

"I was flying by the seat of my pants, while you put your best foot forward. You certainly carried the team." Of course, I was blowing smoke. In this family, that was business as usual.

SIGHTLINE

By Tom Yeoman

MATTY SAT IN the editing bay assembling the footage she'd shot for an interview about a lost dog, then unwound in her chair, letting her work-stress ebb as the TV story began to output onto the station's programming server, the blue progress bar in the dialog box advancing from left to right.

The little girl in the video had been appropriately teary, her father sympathetic and perplexed. Matty knew that Charge, the assignment editor, would smirk at the man's country coffee-shop ways then loudly demand to know if they'd even touch a story like this if they had anything more eventful to program for the channel. Anything even a little more exciting?

That was the immediate problem: lately, the pace

of life here had been really slow. Slow with the grind into a rainy spring, its unrelenting passage ticked in this hour by droplets on the outside glass. Slow enough, she thought, that it was disturbingly possible the little girl holding up the German Shepherd picture for the camera could actually become their lead story for today's local news.

At least, she thought, *we're not covering whose dog had puppies*.

No, there had been an air of genuine mystery in the fact the dog's tracks had come to an abrupt end out in a muddy patch of side road. Old Tweed's disappearance did look inexplicable. And thin though the story was, it could at least be reported on. *Has anyone seen the lost dog?*

It was what she kept hearing about from the trickle of human contacts at the periphery of her social encounters that seemed to defy her role as a community journalist: something with only nebulous detail, but deep in implication. *Life-altering.* And yet intangible, as though it couldn't withstand close scrutiny or open sunlight. But it was disquieting, with more than the grist of her daily reporting.

People reluctantly opened up, and said they had

seen this *something*. They seemed abashed, perhaps embarrassed they'd be laughed at. But they divulged anyway – uncertain as they were on the reception of their stories, these witnesses were still driven by a heightened confessional need...they had to let someone else know.

There was a strongly related factor at play: the *something* provoked an intense, existential fear – no, a gut-locking terror and menace with an intensity "Of magnitudes!" beyond any fear originating with the mundane sources of the region's rolling woodlands. This fear, they were unable to keep to themselves.

Matty felt herself frown. Out the door, beyond the windows at the end of the hall, the foreboding world waited. Under the crumpled contours of rain clouds, the trees had desaturated from green to greys of multiple depths. She reached for a pen and collected herself, then began to write out her thoughts.

The fears of the witnesses centered on an apparition from the forests. They agreed that it was bipedal, tall, "a big grey thing" with glowing chatoyant eyes that burned red with a reflected or, perhaps, an inner glow. Emotional shock, further hurt by poor descriptive abilities, left these everyday witnesses struggling to describe specific details; much about the locations for these sightings made the monster tough to discern closely.

"It was dusk."

"Cloudy and dim up there."

"The light was poor."

"It got me like a deer in the headlights."

"It was under those trees there."

"I didn't see it that close."

"I saw it too close."

Their voices fell, apprehensive, timbered with the edges of night.

Behind those commanding eyes, the mass of its upper body filled out with folded, chiropteran wings that lay across its back. Sometimes it unfolded them, and witnesses jumped back and fled the scene.

Was it an animal? By their descriptions and comparisons, it seemed to combine characteristics or qualities from several different creatures – bat, owl, spider, human – while being absolutely none of them. An alien encounter, then?

Matty thought about this, decided against it. The people did not describe anything in the vein of a person-to-person or intelligence-to-intelligence quality in these encounters at all. The *thing* was flatly unreadable, and did not act or react to them as they did toward it. Almost solely, the victims were the actors, the expressors. The ones who relived their unnatural encounters and disquieted aftermaths. The ones whose memories scarred them.

In whichever area the sightings occurred, the thing seemed to have arrived first for its visitation and been waiting – because, Matty suddenly decided, it *was* waiting: waiting to terrify someone. Yet it seemed strange that the thing, as described, could provoke such depths of negative emotion. *Could that be what it's there for?* Matty mused. There to draw from the fear somehow?

How does that work? She asked herself. Her pen scratched as she struggled for words to these thoughts.

On the screen, the blue bar completed its output, and the dialog box winked off. The vanished dog story now waited in the programming server. That was routine, the stuff of everyday at their channel.

The thoughts came together: *Dog snatched from a muddy road by something that flew. Monster has been seen to unfold bat-like wings and take flight. Was* that *what happened?*

Ah, Matty thought, from her calm epicenter of a burgeoning grey storm-eye. *The greater story's barely been touched…*

SUMMER

Solstice and Scenery

MARLOW

By Amanda Chomiak

SOMETHING ABOUT THE drive through the foggy sea air, which rolled off the water so early in the morning, made him feel alive. The breeze through the driver's side window was still cool, but warmed fast as he tore along the coastal highway in his Ferrari 458 *Speciale*.

The aerodynamic wonder on four twenty-inch wheels was cherry red with blue and white centerline striping over the hood. The car was devastatingly sexy in the dark, but the orange dawn sunlight really showcased its custom paint job.

He'd dropped over three hundred K for this baby and it felt so good to get her out on the open road. The drive down to San Francisco from Portland hadn't taken long at all. He would complain the time passed too quickly, but he had bought a sports car, after all.

When he passed a Jeep full of pretty girls on his right, he couldn't help but smile and run his fingers through his thick, wavy, black hair. There were three brunettes and a sweet but stunning blonde with pigtails behind the wheel. Her top was tight and short and she giggled when he made eye contact with her.

He shot a wink her way and would have loved to hear the bell-like sound of her laughter. He wished she was sitting in the empty carbon-fibre racing seat to his right. He could almost see her delicate, nervous fingertips as they caressed the red stitching, picked at it with her blue-painted nails. He wouldn't even mind. Not for her.

But not now. Not yet.

The Jeep's music faded behind him as he accelerated. The fog had begun to clear, and the view of the rocky coastline below stole his breath. Damn, he'd missed the California coast: the beaches, the heat, and the women.

Oh, the women.

He never failed to find a date out here. His good looks, almost boyish, made him appear younger than his true age by about five years. His car, different every year, but always equally exotic, showcased his wealth better than his bank statement ever could.

Attracting the 'right' woman hadn't been much of a problem, either. In fact, the last six years he had made this trip, she seemed to fall right into his lap each and every time.

He remembered his first. Paige. Delicious, pale skin in a world of spray-on tans stood out like neon lights; blonde extensions; round hips and tiny feet. She reminded him of Marlow. So much so, he'd mistakenly called her by the wrong name.

It didn't much matter in the end, though. Not really. Who would she tell? How could she tell?

But year after year, he seemed to find another replacement. Replacement was a poor word choice, though. Marlow could not be replaced, compared, or equaled. These women, they were just stand-ins for her; actresses who had a role to play. They allowed him to act on a need, on an impulse.

They had all been so willing to follow him, to get into his car. A stranger's car. He'd been told he had a great laugh. So, he would laugh. And they would follow like sweet little lambs with the innocence to match.

But they never quite got it right.

They couldn't match his Marlow; always fell short in some way or another. Too many freckles, not enough. A scar, a tattoo. They just weren't exact. They missed the mark, didn't have that spark, that zest.

His white knuckles on the steering wheel told him he was troubled, again.

He forced a hearty laugh and a pseudo-genuine smile. Even a curt nod at his own reflection in the rear-view mirror helped to calm him. Somewhat. It was summertime in California and he was happy, after all.

But, why, damn it, why was it so hard to find another girl like her? His past failures, and that's what they were, failures, nagged at him.

Paige. Annabelle. Hilary. Beth. Tara. And just last year, Misty.

Their names, like their faces, were burnt into his mind. Branded there behind his sage green eyes. Eyes so clear, he was sure they'd lured as many as his laughter had.

Misty had liked his eyes. She'd complimented their unusual colour. She had stared into them that night with her own unblinking, red-rimmed baby blues.

He heard of others keeping mementos like trophies: a lock of hair, a finger, or toe. But if these girls were wrong, were flawed, were defective in some way, why would he want to commemorate that? It was bad enough Marlow's memory had now been muddied by his attempts to replace her.

But a deep urge to bring her back kept his work alive. It wasn't really work. It was a project. Hell, it was his mission. He owed it to himself to find another as special as she was. One who would make his body react like hers had.

Marlow had captivated him from the first moment she skipped past him on campus. She bloody-well skipped like a little schoolgirl. He'd never seen such lightness, such innocence. Nothing would have made him happier than to capture her and keep her locked away in a glass jar so the evils of the world – greed, lust, temptation, anger – never touched her.

Another human being had never had the ability to draw his attention. Her carefree attitude was refreshing, fascinating. She was a rare beauty who no one else seemed to notice. As far as he could tell, she didn't have a man in her life. A shame for them, but such luck for him.

He would laugh as he watched her in the courtyard on those crisp autumn days. And that laugh, his cursed laugh, drew her to him. The golden yellows and ripe reds swirled around her feet as she stood in front of him and smiled like he was one of the world's wonders. She had been so easily charmed with the right words and a properly placed touch of wit. Too easily charmed. He wanted to feel guilty, but he couldn't.

Once Marlow was his, he didn't let her go. And six years later, he still could not.

He brushed his cheek, expected to catch a tear at her memory, but both hand and cheek were dry. Just like last year and the year before and the year before and the year before and the year before and even the year before that.

He was all those things: all those evils he despised. He wished someone else had found her first, locked her away in a glass jar to protect her. To save her. If they had, she might still be alive.

He was the embodiment of greed, lust, temptation, and anger. He couldn't help himself. He wanted more than she would give or even could give. He needed more. So, he took it. He took it too far.

Then she broke.

A gull screeched overhead, screamed like a scared woman. The piercing sound woke his often still heart. He smiled to himself and was soothed once more by the sound. This year, he thought, this year, he would find himself a new Marlow. One not so fragile.

She was out there, he was sure. And he wouldn't stop his search until she was his.

MOMENTS

By Randy Ward

IT'S A HOT AUGUST afternoon and the salty sweat seeping from my pores drips into my eyes, stinging them.

I continue to push the lawn mower, the type with no motor, just a curved blade cutting the grass.

I'm almost done.

The smell of the freshly mowed grass is intoxicating.

I glance over at my new girlfriend of two months, sitting on the deck wearing a string bikini. Her tanned skin shimmers in the hot August sun. Her face is relaxed as she soaks in the sun's rays like a sponge. The white fabric of her bikini is a stark contrast to her tanned skin.

I should go over there, maybe things would get interesting, I think. The other side of my mind says, *you better not, you know what happened last time! You didn't get any more work done that whole day and almost got your ass fired.*

Something is changing in me. I've never felt this way before. I can't stop thinking about her. The words to an old James Taylor song come to mind, *"I feel fine every time she's around me now, and she's around me now almost all the time."*

My heart flutters just thinking about being in that state; being in love.

Then the fear comes. *What if she doesn't feel the same?*

I look at her again. Her eyes are now open, staring at me like she knew I was staring at her.

"What are you thinking?" she asks.

Should I tell her? Will it scare her off?

My heart thumps. My mind is divided. *Tell her! No don't say anything. Don't ruin it!*

I'm so confused, but her stare is so intense it draws me into her soul.

"What are you thinking?" she asks again.

I drop the handle of the mower and go to her.

A kiss on the lips. The lips are salty and tasty. My hands cup her face.

I know the words won't stay inside, they must come forth, despite the possible repercussion.

The words pour forth, "I'm thinking, I love you! I think about you all the time. I want you, I need you!"

My eyes are locked on hers, which are a deep blue, like the waters of Tobago Bay.

Then I see the change in her. Her body tenses, her eyes sadden and her skin turns cold.

Her voice, usually filled with tenderness is now cold and hard, "You knew when we first started this, I was married. There can't be more than this. This is a diversion for me. Nothing more!"

She takes my hand from her face and walks into the cabin.

My heart aches, my chest feels the weight of the universe. The taste of sorrow floods my mouth.

I'm left standing on the deck staring at the door.

I return to the mower, pick up the handle and cut the grass.

My thoughts are, *I wish I had listened to the other side of my mind and said nothing.*

That moment cost me my happiness, I know things will

never be the same.

MY SADDLE HORSE HAS DIED

By Ken Orich

My saddle horse has died.
My best friend true and tried.
We rode the range together
Through every kind of weather.

Thirty years we relied on each other.
Closer to me than my own brother.
You always knew what I was thinking.
Now you are gone; my heart is sinking.

I remember the first day I saw you,
Trotting 'cross the prairie and that's when I knew
You were the perfect horse for me.
All those other horses, I didn't even see.

First thing first, I had to catch you.
You didn't make it easy – that part's true.
Then we had a three-day rodeo contest
To see which one of us was the best.

I must admit, you had me beat;
A hundred times I landed at your feet.
I think it was the apples that finally did it.
You knew I was never gonna quit.

So that day a deal we made;
An apple to ride you was fair trade.
Every once in a while I forgot to bring you one
And I'd be grabbing air, my feet pointing to the sun!

It took us a few years to work out the kinks.
Remember that time you were spooked by the lynx?
You left me on the prairie all alone.
It took me ten hours to walk home.

But I wasn't mad, I understood.
We were partners through the bad and the good.

For thirty years we were best friends.
It's so sad that this is where it ends.

UNDER A SUMMER SKY

By Sarah Deverall

THE SUMMER BREEZE fluttered the long hair about her face. The earthy brown strands, light, airy, like silk, tickled D'Avid's fingers. He had never touched anything so fine; he felt a sense of tenderness at such fragility.

The fairy sprite glared up at him, her green eyes flashing. He had plucked her from her perch in the Red Lotus tree without so much as a 'by your leave'.

She should have feared him; he was much, much larger than she, yet here she was, eyes spitting fire so he was the one feeling intimidated. He snorted at the absurdity of it. He, the King of D'Vil, afraid of such a tiny being?

"I mean you no harm," he said softly. He lifted his hands, with her cradled in them, so he could look into her deep emerald eyes. She responded with an animalistic growl.

"I seek the Stone of A'Dan. It is sacred to my people and was stolen twelve years ago, by my enemies, leaving my lands barren and infertile."

He and his men had searched hither and yon. They had been led here, to this place, the Fountain of Souls and the Pool of Reflection, by heeding the words of the sages and hags and interpreting the roll of the bones and the patterns in the blood.

He would have missed her had not his familiar, a blue kestrel, alerted him to her presence. Though she had been well camouflaged, he had been able to pluck her from her hiding place among the red lotus blossoms on the tree. She was beautiful: light brown hair, pert little nose, delicate pointed pixie ears, flashing green eyes and a curvaceous body that stood only eight inches. His vision of an ideal woman… if only she were five feet taller.

Even as the thought passed through his head, he felt a shift as she began to grow larger. The weight of her became too much for his cupped hands to hold and he released her, setting her upon her feet before him.

"I am S'Adan, the Keeper of the Stone." She hissed and stomped her tiny foot. She pulled at a thin leather cord around her neck. At the end, dangling between her breasts, was an opal, shimmering with crimson fire. No wonder he had not been able to find it. It had been cradled, safe and warm, protected.

He reached out to take it from her, brushing his knuckles against her ample bosom. She slapped his hand away. "It was lost to my people for many millennia, before I found it again. On your lands."

"I am D'Avid, King of D'Vil." He rubbed his stinging knuckles. "I was told I would find that which I seek and all I desire here, in this place."

He leaned forward to gently lift the pendant from her chest. The opal burned in his hand. "I need it," he whispered.

"The Stone is mine," she declared.

Under a Summer's Sky,

One might find,

A beauty so rare,

With love to share,

The Stone of A'dan

And a Jewel

To lead the clan.

The words of the sage echoed in his ears as he pressed his lips to hers.

His lips started to tingle… then his nose and face. He pulled back to stare at the pixie. Her eyes were closed and she was smiling as she swayed toward him. D'Avid shrugged and pulled her back into his arms and kissed her again, nudging her lips open with his tongue.

S'Adan groaned at the invasion and wrapped her arm around his chest, her hands stroking his shoulders. The stone between them pulsed, where her chest met his.

She frowned as she felt a slight shift in their position. She suddenly felt taller than he.

His kisses moved down her neck and she craned her neck to allow him better access and ignored the change when his arms fell away from her back to her waist.

Sensations of pleasure engulfed her, so much so that she felt the need to pull back lest she be swallowed whole. She opened her eyes to stare at D'Avid but he was no longer in her arms. Where had he gone? What had she done?

D'Avid gazed around him in shock and bewilderment. One minute he was kissing a beautiful maiden and the next, he was standing in a forest of tall, thin green spears.

He peered up to the heavens only to stagger backward in confusion at the giant woman standing over him. He recognized her as the fairy he had been kissing. What spell had she put him under?

THE JERSEY

By Amanda Chomiak

JUNE 29TH, 2017

4:39: I wake up to an alarm blaring. I roll over to discover two things. First, the sound isn't coming from my alarm clock, so I can't silence the noise. And second, I'm not alone in my bed.

5:03: The fire department is parked out front of the complex, red against the red sunrise. I'm sure Mrs. Cavendish in 6F burnt her cat food, or something.

5:18: I'm making an omelet for a beautiful redhead whose name has currently slipped my mind. She does have incredible peaches and cream legs peeking out from under my Canada 150 hockey jersey. Can't complain.

6:27: Charlotte, or Cherri, leaves. Still wearing my

jersey. That, I will complain about. The thing cost me eighty bucks.

7:42: I wake up, again, in a panic. It's not Saturday. Why the heck did I go out on a Wednesday night? Why did I drink that much? Yeah, right, wine is good for you. It's brought me nothing but stress.

8:13: I pull up to the office complex. Thank goodness I only live five blocks away. I'm late, but not so late the senior VP will notice. I carry an armful of files, so naturally I look useful and very, very busy. And Angie has hot coffee on my desk. She is the best.

8:58: I have a date for tonight. Reagan, Mark's secretary from the eleventh floor, has been making eyes at me for the last two months. I decide to put her out of her misery and ask her to drinks. I immediately regret it. I meant to find Cheryl tonight and get my jersey back. Oh, well. There's always the weekend.

10:47: Just stepped out of the meeting from hell. More work. More plans which need to be drawn up. I'm going to need complete silence for at least two hours. There goes lunch. I'll have something brought in.

12:52: Two hours plus five minutes. And no food. I was in the zone and forgot to have Angie bring in Thai. That was a rough project. But as usual, the final product is phenomenal. There's a reason they pay me the big bucks.

1:15: I'm eating lunch with Angie. She's a good assistant. Great actually. She anticipates everything I need. I am certain I couldn't live without her. It's about time I let her know how much I appreciate her hard work. She has red sauce on her cheek and I'm unsure if I should tell her. I don't want to embarrass her. Though she would look beautiful with flushed cheeks. I can't help but smile.

1:17: I was right. Angie has a beautiful blush. And now I want her. I loosen my tie. How have her looks, her allure, eluded me for the last three years? I'll think about this later. Besides, I have drinks at seven with Mark's secretary, Renee. Not Renee. Reagan. But I guess I'm free at nine?

1:46: I'm washing my hands in the bathroom and already regretting asking Angie to a late dinner. She hasn't stopped giggling since I asked her. Up until this point, I hadn't heard her laugh. Bad boss. But really, it's annoying. I hope she doesn't keep it up in the office.

2:00: Another project awaits me on my desk when I return from lunch. I'm certain I'll do an incredible job. Work always takes my mind off women. And really, I know I'm fully to blame for the messes I keep getting myself into. But I just can't help myself.

4:13: Aaron, the senior VP, stops in my office. He's pleased with the Jackson account. Not surprising, but always nice to hear. A good fifty percent of my personality is centered on my ego. It likes to be stroked.

5:18: I'm starving. Angie brings me pastries. She knows about my sweet tooth. It's convenient, and I'm kicking myself harder for asking her out. If she quits or transfers when she finds out I'm not a commitment kind of man, I'm going to be screwed. And not in the good way.

6:50: Reagan shows up at my office looking like every man's fantasy. Low cut blouse, short skirt, high heels. I'm not complaining, but I am. I don't like my personal life parading around my office. Through the open office door, I see Angie heading to the elevators. She usually stays until I leave. Seven. Darn it. She's seen Reagan. And she's mad.

7:04: I'm drinking straight whiskey. Reagan is pleasant, but I'm upset about Angie. I'm also worried I care so much. I might not do relationships, but I'm not a bad guy. At least I try not to be. I'm not in the business of breaking hearts. I can't stop thinking about Angie.

7:22: I'm alone. I called Reagan by Angie's name. It was an honest mistake, and clearly, three drinks in twenty minutes was far too much, far too fast. I scroll through my phone and find a Charlene. She must be the redhead from last night. The photo beside her name is nothing but impressive cleavage, but I think I see red hair over her shoulder.

7:24: Charlene is on her way to the bar with my shirt. I'm happy about that. I hate loose ends. But, still I'm thinking about Angie. I'm nervous for our date. There's a first time for everything. I'm worried she'll stand me up. Again, a first time for everything.

7:45: Charlene is on my lap, laughing, kissing my

neck. She forgot my jersey at her place. Consider me annoyed. I'm worried about her red lipstick. This shirt wasn't cheap. And my dry cleaner will think I'm easy. Obviously I am, but Ronnie is nearing seventy and reminds me of my grandmother. I don't want her to think I'm a bad guy. She always has cookies for me when I pick up my suits.

8:30: I'm leaving Charlene's place, jersey clutched tightly in my hands. She washed it. It smells like flowers and perfume and I'm certain it's a size smaller. Who uses the high heat setting on the dryer? Jerseys are delicate. I'm a man and I know this. Charlene distracted me well enough, but I won't be back. Laundry is serious stuff.

8:31: Angie steps into the elevator. Why is she in Charlene's building? She looks just as surprised to see me. She sees the jersey, the lipstick stain on my collar, and immediately steps back out of the elevator before the door closes. Before I can explain.

8:59: The cab drops me at my house and I shower and change. I know Angie won't be at the bar when I get there, late. But I go anyway. For some insane reason, I want to hear that ridiculous giggle of hers. I am so mad at myself for messing this up. I'm not the kind of guy to care about things like this. But I can't stop the beautiful images of Angie's blush from flashing behind my eyes.

9:20: I'm at the bar. And I'm drinking club soda. Plain. I'm officially an eighty-year-old woman. Someone get me my purse.

9:30: I hear the giggle. Angie's giggle. She's here.

9:35: I approach Angie's table. She's with another guy. He's good-looking enough, but nowhere near as well dressed as I am. I know it's hypocritical of me, but I'm jealous. She's mine. She spends eleven hours a day at my beck and call. I can't get through my days without her. And now I want her evenings, too. Her nights. I don't know what's come over me, but I can't help it.

9:45: Angie is mad. I've scared off her date and am now sitting across from her, but hey, she's still here.

9:55: She smiled. Once in the last ten minutes, but it's something. Ten straight minutes of back-peddling, and I seem to be making progress. I'm not used to this. It's like work. But I think I like it. It's nice to care about someone.

10:15: The sun has set, but it's not deep dark outside as Angie and I walk back to her place. It's nice that I can see her face, her dress, her body. She has warned me this night isn't going to end the way I think it is. And I don't even care. I'm just happy to have her hand in mine.

11:30: I smile down at Angie's head on my bare shoulder. The night turned out exactly how I thought it would. And damn, she's even prettier when she sleeps than when she's keeping me in line at work. I think I might be in love with this girl.

11:59: Yeah. I'm in love with her.

12:37: I get out of bed to turn out the lights, to lock the doors. This is downtown Toronto after all. I walk past the laundry hamper and choke back a laugh. There's a Canada 150 hockey jersey crumpled in a ball next to the pink blouse she wore to work the day before.

My day, the longest day of my life, started with this jersey, and now, it's ended with it. We have more in common than work, it seems. Fate? I think so.

THE HANGING TREE

By Ken Orich

The Hanging Tree is down now.
Its branches crushed and broken.
Lime-green lichens still cling to life
On branches long dead, bleached by sun.

The Hanging Tree is down now.
Crumbling, rotten and broken.
In a meadow full of life
Wildflowers blossom under the sun.

The Hanging Tree is down now.
Snapped off at the root and broken.
Entering the next cycle of life.
Decay aided by wind, rain, and sun.

The Hanging Tree is down now.
Bark peeling off and broken,

Exposing the tunnels of insect life.
Stark gray, feathered green under the sun.

The Hanging Tree is down now.
How long was it there before it was broken.
When did the giant Fir lose its life?
Its needles turned brown under the sun.

The Hanging Tree is down now.
It was dying but not broken,
Lightning strike slowly taking its life.
Branches turning gray under the sun.

The Hanging Tree is down now.
We are sad, heart-broken.
Though long-dead, we saw life.
Our landmark under the sun

The Hanging Tree is down now.
Painted on canvas before it was broken.
Brush Strokes have given back life
To a tree that challenged the sun.

THE GODDESS OF SUMMER

By Randy Ward

I LOOK AROUND the room at a smorgasbord of blondes, brunettes and red heads. A sprinkling of blue and pink heads of hair are scattered throughout the crowd. The dance is in full swing.

Then, I see her. She reminds me of summer. Her bright blue eyes sparkle like the rays of the sun's reflect-ion off a cool blue lake. Her hair looks soft and silky, flowing down to the small of her back.

Her tan is a bright contrast to the white summer dress she is wearing. It fits her perfectly. The yellow flowers painted on her brown sandals match the colour of her painted toe nails.

Who is this woman, this goddess of summer standing tall and lean, looking over the crowd?

I summon the courage from the pit of my stomach

and step toward her.

I notice the slight change in her eyes when she sees me. She watches me like a cop watching a suspect, taking in my gait, my size, my demeanor; analyzing if I'm a threat. I feel her eyes examining my soul, my innermost thoughts. I sense that she knows I'm afraid of her, intimidated by her beauty.

I force my gaze to lock on her piercing blue eyes. I'm close enough to smell her scent. It smells of summer, like lilacs and irises. The smell pierces my brain. I feel euphoric, a lightness I have never felt without the aid of booze or drugs.

As I inhale her intoxicating scent, I manage to force my brain to work enough to say, "Hi." I want to say something witty that will make her laugh, but my brain won't focus my thoughts.

She smiles the smile of angels and says, "That's your best line? Hi?"

I strain to get my brain clear and back under control. "The best line is honesty and I want to meet you, so hi it is." I reply.

She nods slightly and says, "I'm Misty, like a soft rain."

"I'm Sean, like in Sean Connery, you know, James Bond," I say in my best English accent.

She smiles and reaches out her hand. I take it and we walk away from the party together.

"I've held that hand for over 50 years," I say now, to my special granddaughter sitting in front of me on the front porch.

I've told the story of meeting her grandmother many times.

She loves to hear the story over and over.

I tell it to her a least once a month.

I believe her 13-year-old brain finds it comforting and reassuring.

She looks up at me and says, "Grandpa, does your heart ache for her as much as mine does, now that she's gone?" Her face changes to the colour of sadness and tears flow down her beautiful face.

"My lovely girl, I still see her every day in my mind's eye. I see her in your mother, and I see her in you. I know that I will see her again, little one. I will again hold her hand and get lost in her eyes," I say in my most comforting voice.

I take my granddaughter's hand and we both

recall the smells of grandma's cooking coming through the open windows and onto the front porch.

We smile and get lost in the thoughts of that beautiful, caring, intelligent woman once again.

OLD HARD ROAD

By Tom Yeoman

HOT WIND SHIMMERS through the wires hanging in elongated bows from pole to pole along the worn flat-top. The neglected two-lane road, represented on maps as a thin black line, leads into a broad cusp of air ripples rising from a disused bowl of tawny farmland. Trees heave in the brilliant day-wash, their cascading leaves rustling in the call of a great land ocean and out of this grand, agrarian roar, one song lifts.

It's the wind, giving voice to an ordered throng of wires: the thick twined ones highest up connect the tall, spaced-out poles at the top; the lower, lesser barbed ones in lines of three tacked onto fence posts, giving the land a boundary from the road for miles of parallel.

The posts shimmer in the hot sun and begin to

add a cadence to the crack-ticks of the secondary highway, their blur-past a time signature seen from the speedy passage of a vehicle. Their wire-song voices shiver in a fugue of strands and tossing trees, the sound a knife blade or a ring or a small glass or brass cylinder makes on a fret board to give a resonant hollow-body a plaintive call. The wind, a finger from outer reaches, plies the resonances of the land.

How many dreams and how much drama had spilled onto the faded sections and worn patches of this road, a back beat to a backstretch of passing lives? An empty house of sagging weathered boards caught those passions long ago with the full force, then, of the air mass drumming on it now, but now the old house can only do a slight perspective turn behind blurring-tall grass patch of a had-been lawn, before it's engulfed by a stand of skeletal grey trees on the furthest edge of the property. Their voices hiss. Above them, the old strand-lines sigh.

Directly ahead, the road runs straight, rising and dipping modestly with the level of the land. From its perspective centre, the lines of the parallels stream out. There's so much emptiness here, where the humble growth quietly reclaims acres of eroded furrows, lending their own low hiss to the troubadour wind.

Jug-whistle tones carry from an empty eye socket in a cow-skull, a bleached rib-rack fanning out behind it in a rictus that's gone in a blur. There are blues in the back roads, coaxed from lesser choices made too easily, from realities that couldn't cooperate with ambitions. They left imprints. The surroundings too bear the suffering.

In the space of five heartbeats, the vista offers a sad, rusted-out pickup truck, the ruin of a vintage roadster that once raced along this very highway, the tempo of its tires ticking down moments to a destination. The metronome fell into a last downstroke one day and cut off all further momentum. Something that mattered, stopped. The heartbeats pulse by, and the rust is left to its memories. The vocal airstream goes on alone.

That shimmering call of the land can be an elegy: that touch on the strings a last lament, the sound being coaxed like the low cry of a heart, burdened with grief, in its final pause before the dream's collapse.

How many people lived back here? What tensions did they bear away when they departed? Surely a rose-tinted vision would conjure delights from the roll of the land and celebrate the habitations for the time in which they held their own, when the wind brought senses of change and optimism to husbands and wives on the sod-busting enterprise. From their place on the time stream, they looked ahead. It's the blue-tint that looks back now, sorrowed for what can no longer be, and on this road now, sorrow is nearer than hope. One lone bird prints its silhouette against the strung mid-day wire, and its high quavery cry cuts through the wind.

FIRST MEETING

By Bryan L. Beerling

IT CERTAINLY WASN'T D-Day, but for Valerie it did seem like the longest day of her life and yet it wasn't even noon. Maybe it had something to do with not sleeping all night and finally giving up, rolling out of bed at five a.m. Maybe she could catch a nap later was her thinking.

Something Valerie hadn't counted on was every man in the coffee shop furtively sneaking peeks at her. She only hoped she impressed one man and he hadn't appeared, at least not yet.

She checked her watch again and then the clock on the wall. Fifteen minutes early, thirty if you count the fifteen minutes she sat outside in her car mustering up the courage to go in. When she walked in the door she glanced around. Maybe he had come early too. From what she saw of the men inside, she hoped he wasn't one of them.

No, none looked like their pictures. The waitress asked her what she would like but her nervousness made her opt to wait for her companion. For now she sat alone, both hands cradled around a glass of water, the ice long since melted.

Companion: is that what she should call him? A virtual Thesaurus of terms went through her mind but kept coming back to companion. She had never met him in person, only on Skype. Could it be love if they had never met?

She'd loved another man once, but he proved to not be the man she thought she married. Caution consumed her this time. She hoped, not too cautious. She didn't want to scare him away by being too leery. She'd heard of others who had met this way and for most men it seemed to be just a fling.

Is that what Michael expected? she wondered. Was he just coming thinking he would get her in the sack a few times and then disappear?

She looked at his picture she kept on her phone. Handsome but not gorgeous. At least not what some women would think. He was skinny, but no abs like the calendar firemen some girls swooned over. 'Well, maybe he has,' she thought. It was hard to tell with his jacket on.

She went over what she knew about him: Two years older, widowed with a five-year old son, an accountant, almost a foot taller, dark hair, brown eyes, no piercings or tattoos. The reminder of tattoos hit her hard. What would he think when he found out she had a small tattoo? She lied, saying she didn't have any. She felt confident he likely wouldn't even get to see it, at least not right away.

He never asked for nude photos like some of the other online men. He had only seen pictures of her in slacks and blouse, never dressed up like now. Would he even recognize her in a dress and makeup? She glanced around again to see the men still looking at her. She knew from the way they looked and then laughed at each other they were talking about her. At least, that is what she imagined. Hoping to dissuade them, she smoothed her skirt down over her legs and fastened one more button on her blouse.

She smiled thinking her choice of this coffee shop seemed fitting, the opposite end of town from where she lived and normally travelled. That is why she chose to meet here. Plus, the fact it was right on the highway coming into town. She wondered if he had reserved a room upstairs in the hotel like she suggested.

"So you have a place to sleep at night," she told him, and herself, making it clear this would not be a sexual encounter, just a meeting to see if they liked each other as much as they thought.

This had truly been the longest day in her life, at least it seemed that way, even if the clock only edged towards the noon hour. In reality, this day started long ago, ever since he had seen her profile on that dating site. In the hours since getting up, she had kept herself busy cleaning her apartment. She couldn't get it any cleaner than she had for the past three days since knowing he would be coming.

She laughed at herself arranging and rearranging pictures and ornaments only to put them back where they had been in the first place. She didn't even know if he would come to her apartment.

She had tried on more clothes than she remembered owning before settling on what she chose. Even now she questioned if she should have picked something else. If her mother saw her she would have laughed at how nervous she had been for the past few days since agreeing to let Michael come and meet her in person.

Michael joked on Skype the number five hundred was good luck. They were meeting five hundred hours since first saying hello online. They lived five hundred kilometres apart. In all, she counted six different factors of five hundred that resulted in them meeting today.

She peeked at her watch, now another factor, five hundred seconds until their pre-arranged meeting time. She hadn't even thought to ask if his son would be with him.

"Not enough time to turn tail and run," she told herself.

"Is that what you want to do, turn tail and run?" she heard. She knew that voice without looking up.

'Oh, God!' she thought, 'he heard me.'

Slowly, she turned and looked up at him. Should she shake hands, hug him, kiss him on the cheek? Why hadn't she thought of this before?

Michael wrapped his arms around her and pulled her lightly against his chest. She looked up and slipped her arms around him, squeezing softly. He was as skinny as his picture, no pecs or abs. He bent his head down to look at her and she prepared for a kiss. Instead, she felt his lips on her forehead and he let go.

Valerie pulled her arms back. Somewhere they both said they were glad to meet each other finally. Nervously, she sat down, smoothing her skirt over her legs again and looking down at her blouse. She wished she had left the top button undone. What did the men call it: eye-candy?

They stared at each other for a moment before speaking. Michael repeated that he was glad to finally meet her in person. Valerie nodded. "Me too."

Suddenly she realized they were not alone. The waitress stood beside them asking what they would like to drink.

"Just water," Valerie said and waved her half empty glass while Michael ordered an iced tea. The waitress turned and walked away.

Michael busied himself looking through the menu. Valerie realized even though she'd sat there all that time, she hadn't looked at hers. She wondered what she should order, certainly nothing too spicy. Her nervous stomach might not handle it. 'Can't be puking all over the restaurant our first meeting,' she told herself.

After deciding, they ordered a hamburger for

Michael and a salad with dressing on the side for Valerie.

They stared at each other wondering what to say.

Again Michael said, "It is so good to finally meet you."

Valerie sensed he felt as nervous as her. It eased her. Then his hand slid across the table and held hers. Her nervousness soared. She hoped he couldn't sense it.

"There is a lot of things going on at the lake today," Valerie said. "I was thinking we could go for a walk around there and see what is happening."

"That sounds good to me," Michael said. He pulled his hand back as the waitress brought their meals. Valerie was disappointed. Even though his hand on hers had made her nervous, she liked the feeling.

"I hope you wear baseball caps." She reached down to a plastic bag on the chair beside her and handed him a baseball cap. A red Canadian maple leaf showed on the front and Valerie's city name on the brim. Michael took it from her thanking her as he put it on his head.

"I do," he said as he adjusted the size. "In fact, I had one on all the way here but took it off before coming in. It is in the truck." He studied the hat's emblem before putting it on again. "Certainly not as nice as this, though."

As they ate and chatted, learning more about each other, Valerie decided that this longest day waiting for him was worth the wait. Even if nothing developed of it, she was glad she had taken this step. She wondered if, and when, she would get to meet his son.

WHERE THE WILD BERGAMOT GROWS

By Ken Orich

Have you ever walked where the wild Bergamot grows?
On a hillside with mountains near and wild sky above?
Wind in the willows, lonesome call of a dove.
Follow a trail to see where it goes.

Brown-eyed Susans, Goldenrod, Lupines and more
Wildflowers paint the hills in yellow and blue.
Pinks, purples, greens and silvers sparkle with mountain dew.
I walk along the pathway to Heaven's door.

There's more than just the flowers to see.
Chatter of a squirrel, a Yellow Warbler's song.
Hushed rush of the river on a journey so long

These sounds paint the perfect picture for me.

Pungent smell of Juniper fills the air,
As I sit and absorb the view.
Wildflower meadows and river water blue
I sit in Nature's arms without a care.

Time to go, I follow an old cowboy trail
Past lichen-covered rocks and gnarly trees.
A hundred scents dance on the breeze
Only this can be more sacred than the Holy Grail.

THE PEBBLE

By Randy Ward

I REMEMBER THE first time I saw one.

It was 84 years ago. He stood majestically on the hillside watching the wagons in the cool fall air.

He appeared to have a puzzled look on his face, like he was thinking, "What the hell kind of creature are you, and why are you on my land?"

He was so perfect. His brown fur blowing slightly in the mild prairie wind, his stature straight and tall. The slight musky smell of him carried on the wind.

I was in awe, sitting on that wagon seat at the ripe old age of 8 and coming from the big city of Toronto, hundreds of miles east.

I continued to stare at him when the wagon suddenly shook and stopped. My uncle jumped off the back of the wagon and yelled, "Supper."

My uncle had his big Sharps rifle in hand. The Sharps rifle was taller than I was.

Uncle started yelling, "Yahoo!" and he lay himself on the cool ground.

My 8-year-old mind took a minute to realize he was going to shoot it! I couldn't let that happen. It was the first buffalo I'd ever seen. I'd have loved the fresh meat, but this creature was not a deer, it was exceptional. My mind saw drawings of buffalos in books before starting on this wagon train out west, but to see it standing there was inspiring.

I jumped down from the wagon yelling, "No," but my uncle appeared to be deep in concentration, taking slow deep breaths. The black barrel of the Sharps moved slightly up and down.

Time slowed, the rifle barrel stopped moving. I only had a second and I couldn't get there on time.

I stopped, and my head dropped in disappointment and sorrow.

That's when I saw it, a small pebble sitting on the slightly frozen ground.

The stone appeared to glow, at least that what my

8-year-old mind saw.

I grabbed it. It's smooth, cold, weight no more than the buckle on my pants. It fit my small hand perfectly.

My arm went back. I didn't even aim, I just threw.

The rock sailed through the air and I swear I heard it say, "I'm coming for you."

It hit my uncle's head with a loud, "Thud."

The gun fired and the sound echoed into the coulee and spread throughout the prairie.

I looked up and saw dirt kick up near the buffalo's feet.

He missed!

The beautiful creature stood there a second in defiance, and it appeared to shrug its shoulders before sauntering down the hill out of view.

There are three things I remember about that day. First saving that buffalo. Second, the tanning my dad gave me for knocking out my uncle and third, picking up the pebble that I have had with me for 84 years.

The pebble is a constant reminder to me that no matter how small you are, one person can make a difference.

AUTUMN

Haunting and Harvest

CRISPS

By Brock Sansome

THE BRANCHES AND needles pulled at my shirt and shorts, raking across my bare skin as I forced my way through the dense brush. They left thin red marks, like paper cuts, threatening to seep trails of blood.

Danny, or Dan as he liked to be called, forged ahead, swinging the machete he insisted on getting for the trip haphazardly at the defenceless trees. Twigs and leaves burst into the air all around him. I kept my distance, he was like to swing at me if I was stationary long enough.

The smell of sap and freshly hewn saplings over-powered the stench of rotting leaves on the forest floor. We had been making our trail through the evergreens and birch trees for almost four hours and didn't seem to be getting anywhere. The sun was already casting long yellow beams through the trees.

"I thought you said you knew where it was!" I shouted over the din of the thrashing machete.

"I do, it's just been awhile. Hold your horses, enjoy the scenery."

I stared at the thick undergrowth, at the over-hanging branches weaving thin frail arms together. There was nothing to see.

"We should've followed the trail."

"This," Danny spun back to face me, "is our trail." He flashed his machete before him, thrusting it into my face, small leaves and sap hanging from the sharp piece of steel, the remnants of its victims. He looked at the blade, a gleam in his eyes.

"Yep, the real trail would've been better. And why did you buy that?" It was the reason we had such a late start. He insisted on stopping at Bass Pro before leaving and it took until after twelve for him to window shop the store before he finally noticed the sparkling machete.

He spun back around, took an overhead swing, then stopped.

"Holy shit. Check this out. Gross!"

He moved to the side of the newly made trail,

allowing me to step forward and see what the tip of the machete pointed at. A black cat, swollen from the heat, lay dead, bloated with maggots. The small white insects wiggled and squirmed, making it look as if the cat were twitching.

Then the smell hit us. A putrid stench of rotting meat wafted on the breeze. As if on cue, a swarm of flies lifted off the cat and buzzed around, deafening us to every other sound.

"Hey!"

The shout came from behind us; we both jumped and spun. Danny held his trailblazer out like the weapon it was.

At first, we couldn't see who shouted, and then a cackling laugh drew our eyes to a dense raspberry bush. It was an old man, shrouded from the bush, scraggily white hair cascading down his shoulders and chin. His dirty body looked as if it would collapse underneath him. Sores and bruises covered him. His legs were scabbed over from ankle to knee.

"That's mine." A frail finger shot out, pointing to the dead cat. A toothless grin spread over his face.

"Okay," Danny said as he stepped to the side. I

followed his lead

Slowly, the old man crept from the bush with a gaping smile. He shook with every step, bent over near double. He approached the cat and scooped it into his arms, glancing back at us as if we were going to rob him of it. Maggots dripped from the carcass, slipping between his arms to fall to the ground.

"Mine. Mine." He whispered the words, passing beside us and into the raspberry bush. Looking over his shoulder, he winked and disappeared.

"That… was fucking creepy." Danny swung the blade at a limp branch, severing it in two. He spun away, back onto the trail.

"Umm, where's the backpack?" I just noticed, after all this time, his back was bare. Our food, sleeping gear and everything else we had packed was in it and it wasn't on my shoulders.

"I thought you grabbed it!"

"No, you had it. After we stopped to eat..." He had left it where we stopped for a snack, several miles back. "What are we going to do now?"

I wanted to slap him. He drug me out here to find a shack, that most likely wasn't even still standing, that *might* still have a roof in case it rains. "Oh my god, you moron."

"Calm down. We should be there soon. Last time there was a lamp, maybe it'll still be there."

"And when was the last time?" I stomped on the ground, with little else to do.

"A couple of years. Don't worry. We might just have to sleep under the stars tonight." He hacked away at the trees like I wanted to hack at him.

Suddenly, I thought of the old man and had the feeling he was watching us. I scanned the trees, not seeing anything in the failing light. We worked our way through the trees and bushes, Danny slashing at anything that stood in his way. Twenty minutes passed.

"There it is!" Danny shouted, a squeal escaping his mouth.

Over his shoulder I could see a dilapidated shack in its full squalor. One wall had pieces of missing metal siding, rusted from age. The roof had a thick sheet of moss growing over it, covered with leaves and small plants. It slanted to one side, precariously, fighting gravity and time.

"Just as I remembered."

"This place is junk!"

Danny almost ran to it, ignoring me. A small clearing opened around the shack. Tall unkempt grass and saplings surrounded the building. Before I knew it, Danny was inside. I remembered the old man and moved for the building.

As I reached the door, hanging to one side by half a hinge, a bright flaring light erupted inside. I shielded my eyes, stifling my shout of warning. The oil lamp burned harshly, silhouetting Danny against the building's darkness. It was covered in dust and sent up trails of black smoke from its cracked chimney.

The building had the aroma of mildew. The walls were covered in ceiling-to-floor shelves and those were piled high with mason jars. The dim lantern light glinted dully off those not completely covered in dust.

"What are these?" I leaned to get a closer look at the nearest one. Small, reddish-brown discs. Gingerly, I lifted it, and shook. They rattled inside. "Potato chips?" They looked like the larger crumbs at the bottom of a bag of baked potato chips; salt and vinegar.

I set my jar back down just in time to see Danny reaching inside one of the jars. He lifted the chip and sniffed, then stuck out his tongue.

"Uhg, don't. That's disgusting." I cringed.

"They *are* potato chips. These weren't here before." He bit down and I heard the loud crunch as he chewed. "They must be homemade." He grabbed a handful, dropping the metal lid of the jar to the dirt floor.

"That's, that's too much. I-" I gagged.

"They're not bad. Try some. We don't have anything else to eat."

My stomach growled, as if knowing I was going to lie and say I wasn't hungry. Opening the jar I had picked up earlier, I dumped a handful of chips onto my palm. They were misshapen and odd looking, what I guess homemade chips would look like.

I picked one up and raised it to my mouth. Salt, pure salt. Much saltier than anything I had ever eaten before. I cringed and bit down. It didn't shatter, only folded into itself as if it were damp, the bag left open on the counter for too long.

I swallowed and dumped the rest back into the jar. Danny continued munching away, finishing one jar and reaching for another just as a figure appeared in the doorway.

"What are you doing here?" We both jumped from the raspy voice. The old man from the trail smiled as his eyes scanned the room. He started to cackle, a high pitched reel. "Eating?" He laughed again. "I wouldn't be eating that. Is it tasty?" He bent over and scratched his scabbed shin. A trickle of blood started to run down his leg.

Danny set the jar back onto the shelf, dusting his hands on his shirt.

The old man laughed again and scratched his leg. This time the scab came away and fell to the dirt. Picking it up, he licked it then pushed past me, nudging me against one of the glass filled shelves. They clattered behind me.

At the far wall, the jars were mostly empty. Those that were full, had chips of different colours and hues. Reaching for one on the top shelf, the old man cackled again, focused on both of us, then dropped the large scab into the jar and set it back onto the shelf.

I watched Danny wretch and I wanted to do the same.

GO TO SLEEP, YA LITTLE BABY

By Sarah Deverall

GAUZY, WHITE CURTAINS fluttered as a light breeze wafted in through the partially opened window. The bright harvest moon illuminated the gaily painted nursery. Nary a cloud cast a shadow to mar its glow.

I'm too old to be climbing trees and going over balconies, she lamented as she pushed the sash up higher. Entering with a slight stumble she cursed under her breath. Her legs wobbled as she righted herself, and she groaned at the ache in her knees.

Hobbling to the bassinet in the center of the room, she gazed upon the sleeping child, his tiny mouth sucking softly on an equally tiny fist. Babes were so sweet at this age. This one only a few months old was just past the fragile stage, full of that vital energy she needed to survive. Better still, this child was special, for he bore the mark of the stars. She had seen it in the roll of the bones and it was reaffirmed in the flames of the sacred fire. She was blessed to have found him.

He awakened as she stroked her bony finger across his downy cheek. His eyelids fluttered. His blue eyes opened, then squinted, his small nose scrunching before he let out a howl of protest.

"Go to sleep, ya little baby,

Go to sleep, ya little baby,

Your momma's gone away and your daddy's gone to stay.

Didn't leave nobody but the baby"

The baby settled as the old crone hoarsely rasped the lullaby.

Leaning over the wicker bassinet, she smiled, inhaling his sweet smell. With trembling hands, she carefully unwrapped the infant from his swaddling. The baby's pudgy arms and legs kicked with exuberance. One wee hand reached out to grasp a strand of her lank, grey hair, which had loosened from her cap. She tickled his bare belly, eliciting a smile and a giggle.

Running her wizened old hand over his fair head,

the old crone moved to unbutton the front of her gown with the other. Scooping the babe from his blankets she tenderly kissed his tiny fingers. Cradling him with one hand on his back and the other holding his small head she lifted him up to her bare flat chest. Heart to heart, skin to skin, she held him there. He fussed for a moment, nose wrinkling at her unfamiliar scent. She crooned her lullaby; her soft voice soothing him to sleep.

"Go to sleep, ya little baby,
Go to sleep, ya little baby,
You and me and the Devil makes three.
Didn't need no other lovin' baby."

She swayed as she sang, nuzzling and kissing his blond head. The boy sighed, turning his head into her shoulder, sticking his thumb into his mouth, hand still gripping her limp, grey hair. He made a small, sucking sound.

The air stilled, the room chilled. Pudgy fingers loosened their grip on thick, shiny ebony tresses. The sucking motion of the bowed mouth ceased.

Strong arms now lowered the child from her shoulder. She stared at the lifeless porcelain features of the baby, a tear running down her smooth cheek.

Returning him to his bed, she carefully re-swaddled him. Gently, she placed one final kiss on his brow before she re-buttoned the bodice of her dress over high, firm breasts. She whispered a *thank you* as she strode to the open window and nimbly climbed out into the October night.

ROOMIES

By Charles James

WHEN JAKE DIED, his family had forty-eight hours to gather up his things and vacate the semi-private room he had shared with Sam. Jake's daughter put his clothes in garbage bags and cried quietly as the cleaners came in behind her like blue shadows in cotton gowns and latex gloves.

They sprayed every surface with disinfectant, as if Jake had died from new strain of Ebola. Sam could have moved over to Jake's side of the room when they were done. Jake had the window. But Sam stayed where he was. That was Jake's side.

Then it wasn't.

Sam woke up one afternoon after a nap, and there his new roommate was, standing at the window, leaning on a cane. A white oxygen cylinder stood on the floor next to him nestled in a chrome wheeler. Clear plastic tubes ran up behind his back and into a nasal cannula, little puffs of air jetting out with every laboured breath.

Psssht. Psssht. Psssht.

Sam recognized his new roommate's tattoo first, a pinup girl. At first glance she seemed like a busty Marilyn Monroe, eyes half-closed, lips pursed, racy for the time it had been inked. Now it was faded and withered like the skin on which it was drawn, a relic from a different time, art history.

Most people would look at it and think it was a mistake he made when he was young, the kind of permanent blotch most people wished they could erase. On an octogenarian it was a cute mistake that made him human, a mark that might suggest *I was young once too, and dumb.*

Sam saw something in the ink that most people wouldn't. It wasn't a picture of a bust. The woman's arms were severed.

Sam sat right up, his heart suddenly beating harder than it had in the last two years.

It took a moment for the man's name to come to

him, but it came, as if beating back a crowd of memories all vying for a moment in the spotlight. Sam put him away thirty-two years ago. Foster… the Mutilator.

The two of them should not have been put in the same room, or even the same building. There should have been a rule against bunking an ex-con with a retired cop. In fact, there probably was if anyone bothered to look into the operational guidelines within the Shady Hills Retirement and Assisted Living Home.

But those were the kind of rules that got buried in a mountain of documentation. The reality was that rooms in assisted-living facilities were hard to come by. The waiting lists were long. Like seats in a lifeboat, you had to fill them up.

It was possible, Sam supposed, that Foster wouldn't recognize him, hadn't recognized him. Sam arrested him half a lifetime ago. Since then, he had retired from the police force, sailed to Guam, built a dream retirement home, put his son through medical school, and watched his grandkids grow up. He held Agnes's hand through her final cancer-plagued days. He survived a stroke.

The stout detective who'd ratcheted steel cuffs

around Foster's bloody wrists now had skin like crumpled wax paper. His hair was cotton white. He was a hard-boiled egg with a shell that had over time cracked and crumbled off. Now Sam dragged around his left side like it was a cadaver he couldn't put down. Yeah, there was no way Foster would recognize him.

He barely recognized himself.

He considered that Foster might be different now too. The guy had been in a maximum security prison for twenty-five years. Maybe longer, if he'd been classified as a dangerous offender.

But who was he kidding? Foster flayed his victims. He cut their skin off while they were still alive for no other reason than because he liked doing it. Guys like him didn't sit through an anger management program, join AA, find Jesus and come out the revolving door of the justice system rehabilitated. That did happen, occasionally. But guys like Foster thrived when they were surrounded by others with a propensity for violence.

And now that he thought about it, Sam was sure there were stories about Foster on the inside. Stories got back to Sam because cops talk. The blue network was small. About ten years after he'd gone to the penitentiary the guards tossed his cell on a contraband inspection. They found a collection of mummified human fingers under his mattress, seven of them.

Foster hadn't disturbed Jake's bed yet. On the dresser at the foot of the other bed, a few of Foster's things sat in a neat pile: a red sweater, a framed photograph of a young woman (which seemed odd because Sam couldn't recall the man having any family or lover), an F4 phantom model airplane kit, some acrylic paints, paint brushes, glue, and an X-Acto knife like a little chrome pen with a one inch triangular razor embedded on its tip.

Foster was staring out the window at the school across the road. He looked like a dog, waiting for his master to come home.

Psssht. Psssht. Psssht.

Sam had to get out of there.

He moved quietly, and as quickly as he could for a man whose stroke had numbed everything but the pain. Sam slipped first his wonky foot, then his good one into slippers beside his bed. He stood, trying not to make a sound.

The plan was simple. Get out into the lobby. Get

to a phone and call his son, Barry. Barry could get him out of there. He could be moved out and into another home on the other side of town before the end of the day. Foster wouldn't even know who had been in the room with him.

"Mister Kowalski!" All two hundred and seventy-six pounds of Ava the aide came barreling and wheezing into the room. "You can't be out of your chair, Mr. Kowalski. You'll hurt yourself."

Like a kid picking up a distraught puppy, she wrapped her thick arms around him and planted him in a wheelchair.

He glanced at Foster, who hadn't made a move. He made no indication that he'd recognized the name. In fact, he made no move at all.

Sam had to try something though. Maybe Ava could help him. He pointed at Foster and said, "Garden. Garden!"

Somewhere in Sam's stroke-addled brain the connections misfired. *Garden-tiller. Killer.*

He tried again. "Has a bride!" *He has a wife. He has a knife.*

"Oh I'm sorry, Mr. Kowalski. Mrs. Kowalski died two years ago. You know that. And it's too cold to go out into the garden today. Here let me put the television on. It's almost time for my Soaps."

As she reached for the remote, Sam pushed himself up, out of the chair.

"Oh no you don't, Sugar." Ava pushed him back down and clamped a padded restraint around his hips. It fastened on the left side, where he didn't have the articulation to undo it. "You just relax. It's safer for you like this."

He clenched his teeth. With his good hand he grabbed at her white blouse and pulled her close. "Need straw." *Straw-berry. Barry.* He shook his head. "Money. Straw." *Money-loan. Phone. Phone Barry.*

"Oh, Sugar, I'll get you some strawberries." She overpowered his good arm. Like the final moment of an arm-wrestling match, his wrist slammed down to the chair. "You just need to say please is all. No need to get angry." She buckled each wrist into restraints, the faux fur slicked with the greasy sweat of dozens of other residents.

He grit his teeth.

"You haven't even said hello to your roommate yet." Ava stood up. "You doin' okay over there, Mr. Foster?"

Psssht. Psssht. Psssht.

Foster turned around slow, wheeling the oxygen tank as he did. He stared at her for a moment. His lips were purple, like worms freshly washed up on a sidewalk after a summer storm. The veins in his neck were blue and distended. He had to lean on the oxygen dolly just to stay standing.

"I'm fine," he said. He waved to Ava and didn't even look at Sam. He showed off some yellowed teeth in a jagged smile. No mutilators here. "Sugar."

Her cell phone buzzed.

"Ants. Flies. Give me the… money." *Flies, fleas… please give me the phone.*

"Oh, this is Denzel. I ain't supposed to take personal calls at work, but mmm… you won't tell no one will you, Sugar?"

She turned around with the phone to her ear and waddled out of the room with a long and coy, "Heey Baaabiee."

Sam was alone with him again. When he looked up, Foster was staring at him.

Sam fought against the wheelchair's restraints, stretching the leather against the steel bolts that bound it to the frame, pulling until his own skin began to tear, at least on his right wrist where he still had strength. He pulled up at first, trying to open the loop around his wrist large enough that he might worm his hand free. Then he pulled down, trying to reach the push rings in the wheels, but that was too far down.

He still had his right foot though.

Foster carefully leaned his oxygen tank backward. He had to balance himself, wheel the oxygen tank forward, then drop it so the two front feet on the little black rubber stoppers were on the floor. Then he leaned on it like a cane, and shuffled forward a single step.

Psssht. Psssht. Psssht.

At the end of the cycle, Foster had to stop and take a deep breath, his shoulders rising and falling, as if he'd just pushed a piano one step up a staircase.

Sam's instinct was to push backward. But there was no place to go behind him. Jake's bed was on his left. His own bed was on his right. And behind him, a night-stand jutted out from the wall, underneath chrome tubes and transparent hoses – yellow for vacuum, green for oxygen.

He had to go forward, toward Foster.

His hamstring tightened and he dragged himself forward, one big step. Fortunately Ava hadn't set the brakes on the chair. Unfortunately, his wonky left foot dragged on the floor, steering him left, into Jake's bed.

Sweat was already beading under Sam's T-shirt. Foster took another step toward his dresser, toward the knife.

Sam realized he wouldn't beat the guy. Not like this. But he couldn't give up. He'd been conditioned over too many years of training and walking the beat. His body would keep fighting as long as his heart was still beating.

He changed tactics. With a desperate move, Sam leaned and kicked his wheelchair around, facing the night stand. Foster was almost around the bed now. He didn't like having his back to the criminal, but this way, Sam could push.

He lined up the chair and kicked hard, pushing himself all the way down to the end of the bed. He slammed into his own dresser.

Foster was close now. Close enough to touch.

The old con stopped and coughed into a fabric handkerchief. He wiped little bubbles of spit from the corners of his mouth and then stuffed it back into his shirt pocket.

Sam turned. *Almost free.*

Psssht. Psssht. Psssht.

Foster snapped open the box with the little X-Acto knife and picked it up, little tremors in his fingers shaking it.

Sam turned again and lined himself up with the open door. If he could get into the hallway others would see him. He would be safe. He could call Barry.

Foster licked his lips.

Sam pushed, hard, and flung himself back with all the resolve of a paratrooper casting himself free of an airplane. It was a perfect kick. Sam compensated for the friction of his left foot on the floor and the chair actually curled across the room toward the open door.

Until Foster tapped his hand on the large round metal pad, just next to the dresser, the one with the blue wheelchair outlined on it.

The heavy maple door with the little glass window

in it swung closed.

"Seaweed!" Sam shouted. "Seaweed!" *Seaweed! Kelp! Help!*

Psssht. Psssht. Psssht.

Foster rolled the X-Acto knife between a pair of yellowed fingers.

"Shall we begin?"

WINDIGO WIND

By Ken Orich

Sinister wind moving across the desert floor,
Shape-shifting, searching movement and more.
Innocent leaf-shaking breeze
Moves like a ghost through the trees.
Beware the Windigo Wind!

Chorus of crickets is suddenly still,
As fingers of wind leave an icy chill.
Searching, probing, disturbing the night;
Cold air turns to wispy mist under starlight.
Beware the Windigo Wind!

Desert creatures clear a path,
Sensing danger, unholy wrath.

This wind has a presence that's clear,
It's ominous and something to fear.
Beware the Windigo Wind!

Windigo spirit reborn that night
With heart of coyote under new moonlight.
Waiting for October's full Hallowed moon;
The Windigo will be here soon!
Beware the Windigo Wind!

Spirit-breath across the land
Spins and twists, dust devil in the sand;
Taking new shape as power grows.
Seeking life wherever it goes.
Beware the Windigo Wind!

Low-flying raven plucked from flight,
Sacrificed to give the Windigo sight.
Eyes once black have now turned to red
Its eyes are gone as the raven lays dead.
Beware the Windigo Wind!

Dust devil skips along under desert sky,
Leaves turn brown, wither and die.
Energy grows as the Windigo feasts
From the life of trees and desert beasts.
Beware the Windigo Wind!

Heart of coyote and eagle wings
The Windigo Wind whispers and sings.
The path of death has taken its toll;
Time to look for a human soul.
Beware the Windigo Wind!

Dark essence searches the city tonight.
Dream catchers spinning wildly to fight
Off the Windigo terror that draws near.
Only the dream catchers know what to fear.
Beware the Windigo Wind!

The dream catchers have done their job this night;
Protected their dreamers from the Windigo's bite.
Windigo just moves on to dreamers not protected.
It will move right in without being detected.
Beware the Windigo Wind!

Cats are the best host to get to you.
The odds are doubled when you have two.
Black is best, but any color will do.
If you cuddle them, Windigo will get to you.
Beware the Windigo Wind!

Windigo easily finds a place unprotected.
And possesses nine lives undetected.
Just waiting for a cuddle tonight,
Heart of coyote, raven eye, ready to bite!
Beware the Windigo Wind!

YOU'RE NEVER OUT OF THE FIGHT

By Randy Ward

IT SHOULD HURT more.

I should be screaming in pain, but I can't feel it now.

At first it was so intense, my vision blanked, my mind ceased to function, and I collapsed.

I saw the puff of smoke coming from his gun. I felt the blinding pain. I saw him running down the alley, smoke trailing from his gun in the cool autumn air.

No one said he was armed. Dispatch said he ran from the house after assaulting his wife, but there was no mention of a frigging gun!

Damn dispatch for not getting all the information. Now I'm lying in this fucking alley looking up at the stars, feeling the life leave my body.

My breathing slows. It's getting harder to breath. It's harder to suck the air into my lungs.

I've got to get on the radio, warn them he's armed, let them know I'm down, I'm shot!

Shit! I knew this could happen, but I really didn't think it was going to happen to me. I'm good. I'm cautious. I follow procedure!

My mind returns to seeing him at the mouth of the alley, I yelled, "Stop! Police!" Like everyone else to whom I've ever yelled, "Stop! Police," he takes off.

I ran after him and he turned and fired.

I didn't expect him to turn so quick!

What a shot, an inch below my vest.

I am dying for a frigging inch.

My mind tries to grasp the sound, an echo off in the distance, "11-11 respond. 11-11 this is Base, respond."

I've got to move. I've got to warn my partners, he's armed. I've got to let them know!

Does my arm work? I can feel the blood on it, that must mean it's working.

Try and concentrate; make your arm move," I command my brain. There, it's moving. It's unreal, like it's not me. I see my hand grasp the mic. "Base, it's 11-11, I'm down,

I'm shot."

My hand releases the mic.

My mind starts to wander. It's hard to concentrate.

I hear the concern, the urgency in the dispatcher's voice in the radio bud in my ear. "All unit's head to 11-11's location. He's down. He's hurt. He's been shot."

My hand squeezes the mic again.

"Base, the suspect, armed with a handgun. Last seen running north in the alley at 13th Street."

My thoughts return to me, *I'm dying, and my training still comes through.* A surge of pride courses through me.

I can hear them now. The sirens are off in the distance, getting ever louder. The roar of the engines scream as they race to get to me, their brother.

Breathing is harder now. I take short, gulping breaths. It's tough to focus, difficult to concentrate.

I stare up at the night stars, in all their autumn splendor.

Look at how beautiful the stars are.

Flashes of my life roll through my mind and thoughts of all the things I've left undone.

I'm not done! I want to see my grandchildren graduate. I

want to see my granddaughter walk down the aisle. I want to dance with her at her wedding.

I don't want my wife of 40 years to suffer. I don't want her to have that empty expression of shock and sorrow I've seen on the other wives of my brothers in uniform, when they stared at the casket and got handed the folded flag.

"Breathe," I command, and my voice echoes down the alley.

The air flows into my lungs. My mind says, *the breath of life.*

"Fight," I yell into darkness.

I hear the police cruiser slide on the gravel in the alley. My partner's voice, "Don't you die on me. Fight my friend, live!"

I hear him yell into the radio, "Base get me an ambulance fast! He's semi-conscious, bleeding badly. Get me an ambulance!"

I feel his hands pressing into the hole in my stomach, trying to stop the bleeding

The thoughts return, *I have things left undone.*

In my mind I see my old sergeant in the military, "*Get the fuck up soldier! You are never out of the fight!*"

My eyes open. They focus on my brother kneeling

over me, tears flowing down his face.

"I see you! I have things left to do! I'm never out of the fight," I scream at him.

"Damn right! Fight!" he says, as he is pushed back by the paramedics that have just arrived.

"You're going to make it," says the young life saver working on me.

I bet he always says that, I think.

"Fucking right. I have things left undone," I shout as he puts the intravenous needle in my arm.

I'm never out of the fight.

My mind repeats that mantra, over and over as they load me into the ambulance.

I'm going to be back on the street again. You're never out of the fight.

SIX PACK

By Bryan L. Beerling

THE SIX PACK of beer sat on the closet floor. Well maybe it should be called a five pack. Only five bottles remained in the box, the other in his hand.

Dave's grip tightened, his mouth watering as he looked back and forth between the bottle in his hand and those in the closet. Eight years the box sat there without being touched but it always played with his mind. Some days it was a reminder he did not drink. Other days it seemed an almost unbearable temptation. Almost eight years ago to the day he had put it in the closet promising never to touch it.

"Touch that and I'll walk out the door," his wife had said as he walked in the door three hours late for supper after a hard day at work, and a stop at his favorite watering hole. He tried to lie that he worked late but the look on her face told him she didn't believe him. He shouldn't have even driven home but like always, he did.

He'd heard the threat so many times but her voice seemed different that time. He knew he was an alcoholic, no, more correctly, a drunk. He thought she'd be satisfied he only brought home a six pack, normally it would have been a dozen, not counting what he'd already had in the bar, or sometimes while driving home.

Dave couldn't remember how many times he'd promised to stop drinking but something would happen and a bottle of beer made the turmoil in his life vanish. He never admitted that the one bottle led to another and another before the problems vanished.

A nice cold beer while outside standing at the BBQ always seemed the best. By the time the steaks were ready it would have been three or more and then the fights started. Petty little things would make him fly off the handle and the nice relaxing day would be ruined again.

When she threatened that time he walked straight past her and put it in the closet instead of his usual ignoring her and placing it in the fridge in his Man Cave in the basement. It became a constant reminder every morning as he got his clothes from the closet he promised to never drink again.

Oh there had been many times he had to fight off the urge. The time he ran into an old school-hood friend seemed to be the worst.

"Let's go for a beer," his friend suggested. Dave alibied he had an appointment. But it weighed on him for days. He could almost taste the cold fluid running down his throat. His mouth would salivate and he almost stopped at a bar several times, once even stepping inside, but each time remembering his wife's threat and walked past the door, often quickening his pace.

Once by accident he ordered a beer in a restaurant with his meal. He laughed at his wife's expression. Carefully, he pushed it aside almost out of reach but would reach for it teasingly and then grab a pack of sugar or ketchup instead. Each time his wife would glare and he would laugh.

Sex that night was the best of his marriage, even better than the night she threatened him. It must have been. Nine months later she laid on a hospital bed screaming and pushing out their twin daughters.

Since then it had been easier ignoring the urge. As his daughters grew he found it easy to get over rough times. Their smile was his cure.

As the girls grew he knew he could beat the urge but yet, kept that six pack untouched in the closet.

One time his wife even said he could have a drink when they were out celebrating their 10th anniversary. He didn't know if it was a test or she figured it was safe. He did have a drink: Canada Dry on the rocks.

Dave knew the bottle in his hand would be warm and old yet sensed it tasted as good as one right out of the fridge. With his other hand Dave reached up to his neck and loosened his tie. He slid his arm out of the sleeve of his suit jacket, still holding the beer, then the other arm and tossed the jacket onto the empty bed, still not made.

With his empty hand he picked up the box and carried it out of the bedroom to his Man Cave. He dropped it on the table beside his favorite lounge chair as he slumped between the large armrests. He flicked on the television. It didn't matter what came on, he stared at the bottle in his hand.

Five minutes passed, then another five before he reached for the bottle cap with his other hand. Cupping his fingers around the cap he gripped it tightly to twist it off. He dropped the cap in the box and raised the bottle to his mouth. A noise distracted him and he looked back at the stairway, still gripping the bottle, still holding it to his mouth. Quickly he pulled the bottle away and pushed himself to his feet grabbing the box with the other hand.

Hurriedly he went to the laundry room. As he heard the tiny footsteps coming down the stairway he turned the bottle upside down, holding it over the drain in the floor. He worked on the third bottle as his five year old daughters called out to him.

"Just a minute," he called but that only told them where to find him. They burst through the doorway running to him, each wrapping their tiny arms around his legs. Without looking he knew Sylvia held his left leg, Sally, the other. That is the way they always did. When they were younger it was his way of telling which was which.

Dave looked up to see his sister-in-law at the doorway. Instead of looking at him she looked at the drain and the last of the six pack disappearing.

He looked back at her, speechless, then glanced down at his daughters, both in their best dresses. His sister-in-law had a black dress on. All three looked amazingly alike. All three like his wife. But then why shouldn't they. She and his wife were twins. The daughters were from his wife.

"Daddy," Sylvia asked, "Aunt Theresa says mommy is already in heaven. Is that right?"

Dave looked down at his daughters as he put the last empty bottle in the box and picked up each girl holding them tight, kissing each cheek, part of a ritual he had come to love after coming home from work.

"That's right," he said as he kissed their foreheads. "No more pain."

He looked at his sister-in-law still talking to the girls, "I think Aunt Theresa should take us for ice cream."

FALLING OUT

By Tom Yeoman

FALLING? BUT IT was still summer! A summer fading, with its events passing, a rising time which faced its ebb. Yes, once per year, though this year's summer is still strong and parching, an arid stretch of time full in its moment, yet receding... Amazing, how all of life is past work and play.

What waits ahead is *tempus incognita*, yet when it unfolds, it becomes events within a mostly predictable pattern, and we largely know it already.

So let the routine fall behind us. When we rise, pressures fall. *Particle tracks flare and fade, and fall farther and farther behind.* Ahead, the open skyward abyss flares with unbounded possibility, its openness an exhilarating promise. Wide open! Creativity's dazzling overture through the mind's eye to the pounding heart...

An unseen peril waits: giddy intoxication, winnowing oxygen from the brain, inducing one bliss-out trip into the hard velocity of a long fall. First, a biting stratospheric chill -- then falling, down into the atmospheric gradients, the pressure rising as the windburn thickens to terminal velocity, and the unyielding face of the Earth waits to claim its arriving child in one final impact. Real falls are, yes, that hard.

Falling, like this year's leaves are going to, their own chlorophyll-death begun by the tilting Earth and falling Sun... a between-time of Celtic mysticism, where separate spheres touch so portals between them open, when the inhabitants of each sphere might encounter the beings in others. Beyond such interconnections waits the expectation that the order of the seasons will bring back the Sun, climbing once again, and with its restoration, the renewed echoes of a fervent ancient hope that this year again, the sky will not fall.

Falling, as the Earth itself does in a long, gently elliptical track – falling along a course preset by its own mass and the Sun's powerful pull – a long, lasting fall, far down time's corridors into Sir Isaac Newton's sudden understanding and astronomy's ways of anticipating – then its ability to really comprehend – how the physical cosmos works. Yet the reach of our best minds falls short of the full picture: new discoveries open so much new mystery! And these daring mortals find themselves falling into despair at how far humanity is from resolving it all. There will be mysteries for every age. And there are pieces that, here and now, still won't fit – and the frustrations with them outlast our moment.

Where we need to rise, instead we fall: to long ruts of habit, to inertia, to the ease which defers exertion. The writer's resolve is never far from where procrastination seductively attires itself as as a comfortable moment's rest, easily enveloping the unwary soul: just a moment's pause, an "I'm so tired," and then we fall. Outside that plush, anæsthetizing cocoon, opportunity flits by – opportunity, with its face veiled, its feet winged, its presence fleeting by so quick – here... gone. Did we notice?

What we notice are the leaves changing colour. Fall encroaches through the fading ambient heat and the smoky air, yellow leaves begin to outnumber the green, and we're too tired, maybe too accepting, to rail against the dying of the summer warmth, the passing into the coolness, and cold, and chill. A minus sign for your preferred temperature? It's falling…

SAY GOODNIGHT, BUTTERCUP

By Leslie Johnson

FIVE YEAR OLD Lisa crawled into her bed, hugging a soft teddy bear to her chest as her mother pulled the covers up tight to her chin. "Make sure Buttercup and Cuddles are tucked in too, Momma." She implored.

Her mother, Norah, reached behind the girl and tucked the other two stuffed teddies under the covers. Lisa couldn't bear the thought of either of them being alone and scared – especially in this new house. Everything here was strange and unsettling.

Norah stepped to the door and switched off the light. Lisa looked at her mother's silhouette and wished she had the courage to ask her to stay. Maybe she could sleep in the second bed in her room? She could ask. But she knew she was meant to be a big girl - she was supposed to be strong. So she stuffed her fear deeper as she hugged Fuzzy Wuzzy closer. Her gaze fell to the empty bed in her room.

The door slowly closed and the room dropped into darkness. For a few minutes she let her fear churn up her emotions. She reached behind her and pulled Buttercup and Cuddles under the covers in front of her, all three fluffy friends squashed into her tight embrace. Comforted by their presence she allowed sleep to catch up to her and she drifted off.

The sun felt warm on her face as Lisa rode her horse toward the barn. She loved Paddy, her big bay gelding. Leaning forward, she lay down across his neck, dropping her arms down to hug him. Sitting up, she encouraged her horse to step into the barn. She knew she was supposed to lead him in, but she preferred using the manger to dismount since the ground was a long way down.

In the center of the barn, horse and rider stood for a moment before the floor opened up beneath them. Hurdling downward, they crashed through one floor, then another and another. Lisa lost count as their momentum quickened.

When they finally stopped falling, they were in a dark pit, seemingly unscathed. It was very dark this far down into the earth so it took time for her eyes to adjust. A minute or two later, finally able to discern her surroundings, she knew there was no way out. The room looked just like the barn she'd ridden into except there were no doors. If they were going to get out, they were going to have to go back the way they had come. The gaping hole above her head was ten feet from the ground. That would only get her to the first floor if she could reach it. Looking up she knew that standing on Paddy's back wouldn't help her. And even if she could, she wasn't going to leave Paddy behind by himself.

With a shudder and a muffled scream, Lisa awoke. It was the fourth time she'd had that dream. Laying there, her heart pounding in her ears, she slowly opened her eyes. The hair on her arms stood on end as she saw an orange glow at the foot of her bed. It looked like the glow of a fire without the flicker of flames. When she sat up she knocked Buttercup toward the light.

Her heart skittered in her chest. She didn't know what was happening, but everything in her was screaming -- RUN! Buttercup lay exposed near the foot of the bed.

She needed to rescue him. She wasn't going to leave him behind when she ran for safety.

Rising to her knees she reached out to grab him just as a shadowy black arm slithered out from the orange glow and snatched the teddy bear. Lisa scurried after him, reaching for one of his stubby little legs. A sob broke free as he was dragged off the bed and out of sight.

"Buttercup!" Scrambling to the edge of the bed, she looked down into a pit. It seemed to go on as far as her eyes could see. There in the bottom, stood a horse and rider. The horse edged nervously in a circle - the little girl clinging to his neck and sobbing quietly. She didn't know how – but she knew she was seeing herself in her dream.

She forgot about her lost teddy bear and the dark arm that had snatched him off her bed. She stared at her lost self as she slipped her feet over the edge. There had to be a way to help herself. She bent over, looking for a way down. There was nothing visible, the walls of the shaft seemed to be hidden behind a misty fog, veiled from her sight. Suddenly, two arms reached out of the depths and grabbed her ankles. She screamed and kicked but it was no use. Those cold hands held fast and began to pull her off the bed.

Still shrieking, she twisted onto her belly and grabbed hold of the covers trying to pull herself toward to head of the bed. The blankets proved useless as they gave way. The shadowy arms pulled her off the bed, the covers falling down on top of her.

Landing hard, Lisa wailed at the top of her lungs. Moments later, her mother was there, hauling her off the floor and holding her in a tight embrace. As her fear began to subside, she quieted enough for her mother to lay her back down. Then Norah yanked the covers off the floor and placed them back on the bed, covering her young daughter. Buttercup, lay where he'd fallen near the foot of the bed and Lisa hugged him close to her chest when her mother retrieved him.

It was a dream – it was all a dream, Lisa told her-self as she curled her tiny body around her three fluffy friends. Her mother tucked the covers tight around her before stroking Lisa's soft hair off her forehead. Bending over for a quick kiss, neither noticed the long shadowy fingers slithering out of sight under the bed.

THE RED ROSE

By Amanda Chomiak

I WAS TO MEET her at the bar. She would have a red rose in her hair.

After spending an embarrassing amount of time showering and getting ready, I had to walk briskly up the leaf-littered and overcrowded street to make the nine o'clock date.

I hadn't been this nervous to meet up with a girl since I was in high school and had to deal with the too firm handshakes of the fathers, the looks that kept your hands in your pockets and your libido in the deep freeze.

Rebeccah was something special, though. I had to do this night right. I didn't want to scare her off, as I knew I would not be able to replace her. She was not just another fish in the sea. She was rare. And I wanted her to be mine.

Not in a creepy way, a lock her in the basement kind of possession. Definitely a relationship, which was strange coming from a one-night-stand kind of guy.

This girl was bringing out my romantic side.

I had only met her once. And our first meeting story was one for the grandchildren.

It was a haunted walking tour of old St. Augustine. I had been talked into attending by a few of my college buddies. I should have known they wouldn't show. They were flakes to highest degree, and were probably distracted by a pretty girl, or more likely a frosty glass of beer served by a pretty girl.

But I'd bought my ticket, so I followed through with the ghost walk. It turned out to be more informative and mildly entertaining than it was scary, but overall a good time. Surprising, considering the two families with small children and the elderly couple from Canada I was spending the evening with.

"Sorority chicks always take these tours," Ryan had said over pizza last week. He was drunk when he said it, but I must have been two beers ahead of him as that had been the selling point of the tour for me.

The ghost walk took a promising turn at the cemetery. At first glance, I thought the pale, dark-haired beauty was part of the show, a co-ed hired to scare the paying crowd. Not to sound like a pansy, but when she approached, the moment was ethereal, her beauty haunting.

It turned out her name was Rebeccah and she was a waitress at the Peg-Leg, a cheesy pirate-themed bar on 39th and Main. She wasn't a paid ghoul, either. Just late, as she couldn't find a cab, or something.

She was quiet. Sweet in a way most girls who are hit on for a living aren't. But she seemed to like me, stayed close to me throughout the ghost walk. The feeling was more than mutual.

When the tour ended, she whispered in my ear, invited me to meet her at some dark dive across town on Halloween night.

Based on the long, gauzy black dress she had worn to the ghost tour, you would think she dressed for the holiday year-round. But hey, Goth chicks needed love, too.

After I smoothed the non-existent wrinkles from my sweater, I entered the bar. I spotted her immediately.

Her back to the door, sitting alone in a dark corner. The red rose in Rebeccah's hair was my lure and I took the bait like a starving trout.

I was nervous. And because I knew she would be, too, I decided to skip the small talk and get right to the point. I pressed my hungry lips to her shoulder. Kissed a path up to her ear and because I couldn't resist, nipped at her lobe.

She hummed, and I took that to be a request for more. I kissed the corner of her mouth and only wished I could see her face, her eyes when she turned to meet my mouth with hers.

Why was it so dark in here? It was almost as if we were cloaked in our own little world. I looked over my shoulder and realized I was alone in the room. The rest of the crowd had vanished into the fog which seemed to be swirling around my ankles. The building looked different, too. Old. Like historically old, not just retro.

Rebeccah's cold fingers turned my face and when she deepened the kiss, the ability to think, to rationalize what was happening, disappeared along with everyone else.

And after my thoughts, my breath was next to be

taken. Not just from the kiss, but because Rebeccah seemed to be inhaling it right from my lungs. But it felt deeper than that. Beyond just oxygen. It was like my soul was being torn from my body, from the inside out.

Call me stupid, but I didn't want her to stop.

I was certain I blacked out, even more certain she thought I was dead. But I watched her dress swish above the floor, fog where her feet should be. I heard her laughing with another man.

I rolled onto my back and looked up. A man, dressed in a grey wool uniform was holding her close, as if she belonged to him. Through bleary eyes, I watched them kiss, watched a light pass between their lips.

And then they were gone.

Two weeks passed before I woke up in the hospital with a crazy story to tell.

The doctors thought I was drunk, passed out, and hit my head. No one bought my story.

Except the one nurse who comes to check on me at night. Her uniform seems a little out of date, but boy does she fill it out nicely. She told me tonight, she'll break me out of here. I can't wait to see where she takes me.

FALLING DOWN, IN, OUT

By Vanessa Rieswyk

Falling down

Falling down

Falling down

You can fall down stairs, trees, bed, a hill

Falling in

Falling in

Falling in

People and animals fall in holes,

cars, vans, trucks,

boats, lakes, ponds, rivers and oceans

Falling off

Falling off

Falling off

The leaves fall off trees, people and animals

Falling in and out of love
Falling in and out of love
Falling in and out of love
Girls fall in love with boys, girls and both
Boys fall in love with girls, boys and both
Women fall in love with men, women and both
Men fall in love with women, men and both
Some girls, boys, women and men fall in love with themselves
Girls, boys, women, and men fall out of love with each other and with themselves
Falling down
Falling in
Falling off
Falling in and out of love

AN UNATTENDED SHADOW

By Megan Fennell

IT IS GENERALLY understood there are some things one does not buy secondhand. A toothbrush. A mattress. Undergarments. A coffin. Even the concept of second-hand socks may elicit a particular crawling of the skin.

Now why shouldn't a mirror be counted among these items?

A mirror used for any length of time has seen its owner at their most vulnerable, unkempt and unsure, bleary-eyed and disheveled, primping and preening. It has seen them through the early morning fussing and the late-night hollow-eyed stares of self-loathing. It has born witness to the most desperate murmurs: 'My god, my god, what has time made of me? When I did become an old man?'

I tell you now, that focused emotion which is reserved for one's self above all others sinks into the smooth surface like a fishing lure slipped into still waters, and there the sharp hook remains. A pair of socks may be bleached and washed. How can you scrub the memories from a mirror?

Oh, don't look so distraught. I didn't know any better either.

IT WAS A MAJESTIC thing, my secondhand mirror, a hidden treasure in the trash-heap of the downtown flea market. The gilded frame curling around the edge had a whiff of the baroque about it and the oval surface shone like a newly minted coin. It was the kind of piece that straddled the line between prestige and pretension with reckless nonchalance. A focal piece, as my mother would have said; a piece to tie a room together.

A single nail and a bit of wire was enough to hang it. It fell perfectly straight without the slightest bit of fussing, brightening the bland monotony of my master bedroom, reflecting the sparse sunlight and drawing the eye. I recall thinking to myself, "Now what's all this chatter about the necessity of a woman's touch? Rupert, old boy, I do believe you've got this business of decorating well in hand."

The mirror was the last thing I looked at that night before surrendering myself to the pillow, so it was really no great wonder that it should creep into my sleeping thoughts. I dreamed of silent shapes moving darkly under the surface of the glass, too intangible to name, but bearing with them a shock of helpless dread like looking down into a muddied river and seeing the shadow of piranha teaming suddenly around your legs.

I sat up with a jolt, filmed with cold sweat, temples locked in the vise of a rising migraine. For a moment, I was not convinced I was awake yet. As a matter of fact, as I stumbled into the en suite in search of painkillers, fighting down nausea at every step, I could not be certain whether I'd ever truly been asleep at all.

WITH SUCH AN inauspicious start, the mirror began to trouble me in the daylight hours as well. Passing by it, I would often catch a glimpse of something... wrong. Once while straightening my tie, I thought that I witnessed a grotesque lengthening of my limbs, as though I'd been stretched on a medieval rack. My spidery fingers skittered across my chest in reflexive alarm, and then the image was gone. Another time, leaning close to remove a speck of dust from my eye, I thought that I saw a flash of the socket replaced suddenly with a bleeding hollow. On several occasions, I beheld the flicker of a second presence in the bedroom, standing just behind my shoulder.

So why did I not dispose of the thing? Well, none of these gruesome glimpses ever remained long enough to give me cause to believe in anything other than my own exhaustion. Maybe I had been working too hard yet again. It had become a matter of pride by then, in any case. If I allowed myself to admit there was something truly wrong with the mirror, then I had to admit I had brought this wretched thing into the sanctity of my home, into my very bedroom. I held fast to the idea that so long as I did not believe it had any power to do more than startle me, I could not be harmed.

It was rather like the way children cover their eyes and imagine they are invisible. But when confronted with inexplicable horror, does a grown man too not tend to hide his eyes?

I digress. And I certainly don't want to bore you. You should stop trying to talk. I'm afraid I can't make out anything you're saying, my dear.

NIGHT UPON NIGHT, the dreams of strange movement within the mirror plagued me, and night upon night they worsened. Sleep grew illusive as I shunned the master bedroom, telling myself I preferred to drowse on the living room sofa, an unread novel wilting in my hand.

But even there, I would sink into the fog of half-sleep with a curious sound teasing at my ears. The steady click of a hard-soled shoe on a tiled floor, echoing as though someone was approaching down the length of an endless hallway. I assured myself it was the clock on the mantel I was hearing, even when the sounds fell out of step, overlapping only to separate again. Even when I knew damned well that the sound was not coming from the mantel at all, but from behind the closed door of the master bedroom.

In a final fit of midnight logic, when I truly believed I was being driven mad for some unspecified sin, I summoned my nerve and stormed the bedroom. I threw a black tablecloth over the wretched mirror, lovely frame and all, and stood back to admire my handiwork.

It looks as though the household is in mourning now, my

exhaustion-addled mind supplied. *They cover the mirrors, so that the spirit isn't trapped...*

As though incited by my thought, there came a sudden ripple from beneath the dark cloth. My breath lodged in my throat. As I stared, the material bulged and stretched outwards, distended by the shape of a single hand pressing through from behind it, groping out blindly, reaching for me. The fingers began to twist into the cloth, grasping as though it meant to pull the covering away from the mirror.

My breath exploded from me in a strangled yell and I lunged forward. Tearing the cloth away from the mirror, I flinched violently, confronted by my own stricken face in the half-light. My skin was white and sweating, my teeth bared in a rictus of purest fear. I had never seen myself look so very inhuman, but this was no illusion. The mirror had driven me to this state.

The cloth fell in a heap by my feet as I stepped forward and reached out my hand, driven by some compulsion to ensure the solidity of the mirror. My fingertips skimmed the smooth glass. There was a moment of giddy relief just before my wrist was seized in a bone-crushing grasp. Pulled violently forward, I lost my balance and plunged towards the mirror, then into it, *through* it...

The hand locked with demon strength around my wrist clawed up my arm, jagged nails digging into my skin as this creature within the mirror clambered over me. Like a drowning swimmer, it dragged me under as it pulled itself out, and then I could see nothing, could sense nothing. Silent darkness surrounded me, so complete I would have believed myself dead if my heart had not still been pounding in my chest and my breath not hitching in half-sobs.

When I turned, I could see her there, standing before the mirror. Her dress was ragged and she had the look of long illness about her, but she was smiling. I threw myself against the barrier between us, just as you are doing now, and found there would be no escaping that way. Not without the kind of bridge which my own body had provided for her.

When she raised her hand in farewell, my blood was still dark beneath her nails, and when the reality of my situation struck me with the swift inevitability of a guillotine blade falling, it was then that I found the voice to scream.

So that is my story. And now it is yours. Oh, don't weep. You have as much of a chance to claw your way out as I ever did and at least I was kind enough to explain it to you. I'm sure you think me terribly rude to leave you this way, but you must understand that it's been forty years. This is not a matter of revenge, merely freedom. Begging your pardon, I intend to go outside and stretch my legs.

THE RED LADY

By Shannon Still (L.K. Winters)

RAGE SEETHED FROM Beth's crocus blue eyes, distorting her image in the cracked mirror. The silver-laced glass rippled and peeled from the heat. Soft autumn gold ringlets fell from a perfect French twist and bounced with the tremors of her body. This day had come again. When would she find peace?

Sixty years had passed, the world changing around her. The youthful eyes that stared back at her should have held the wisdom of an old woman whose children had children of their own. But he had taken those gifts away from her, the boy with the alluring hazel eyes. Those eyes belied his true intention, while his mouth whispered honey-dipped compliments.

Beth moved to the window. Her ebony heeled

shoes made no sound in the empty room - her room.

Discarded and broken furniture lay scattered and unwanted, her treasures broken or thrown away. The bright ruby dress she wore, which she'd begged her father to buy for the Valentine's Day dance, was a constant echo of the vibrancy of what the room once was. It flared gradually from her hips to her knees like a cloud over crisp crinoline, still as new as when she had first seen it. She loathed it now.

Outside, the dry grass under the moonlight peek-ed through the melting snow. The house had fallen into disrepair, with each owner that had moved out, unable to abide her. It was better that way. They were a constant reminder of what had been taken from her.

Moonlight crept through the window, gathering dust to its light. Beth's gaze followed the path to the moon and watched as thick white rivers flowed into the milky pool. Anguished faces carried within that river, res-titution unfulfilled, pushed forward against an invisible barrier. Once caught, there was no escaping the moon's greed. Their tormented cries could only be heard by the ethereal world and it pierced her heart.

She moved away from the window to escape their

cries, but they stayed with her. She would not become like them. Retribution would be hers.

The river in the sky was much like the frozen river where her hazel-eyed boy had kissed her and tried to do so much more. Beth had fought his advances, watching him become angrier with each effort of resistance. The indents of his fingertips still haunted her ghostly flesh where he had grabbed her shoulders, thrown her down to the ground.

She reached up to touch the back of her head where it had hit the rock. Phantom pain throbbed. She wrapped her arms around herself for comfort, where rough hands had struggled to pick her barely conscious body up before throwing her into the icy river. Frozen tipped swords had stabbed at her lungs, releasing the last breath of air.

Numbness had slowly freed her nerves from pain, though not before the sharp edges of ice sliced her skin as she was carried off and swallowed up by the river. Something had awakened inside her, urging her to un-tangle herself from the cold currents that would drag her to the darkest depths. The currents jerked her back, not wanting to release her. Clawing at the ice above, she fought the river's pull, finding a hole and grasping the thick edge. With the last of her strength she had pulled herself up, kicking off the cold hands that would drag her down. She grasped at the brush on the bank. Heaving her drenched body away from the water, she searched for her hazel-eyed boy; he was nowhere to be seen.

Beth didn't know she was dead then. Only when the sickening glimpse of bright ruby red material, entangled in a fallen branch, and her very own lifeless crocus blue eyes peeked up at her through wet golden tresses, did she know. Her scream knocked her to the ground. Denial sparked her feet to move toward home, to the safety of her parents' arms.

No open arms would comfort her. Her parents sat comfortably on the couch watching the television, waiting for her to come home as they usually did when she went out. Despite all her attempts to tell and show them she was there, they could not see her. Tears laced with despair fell to the ground.

Time tick-tocked to the hour when she was supposed to return and her parents watched eagerly. An hour passed and then another. Still they waited. This was not like 'Our Beth', her mother had said, becoming agitated with worry despite her father's attempts to calm her. Beth could see by the fear creeping into his eyes that he was worried too. She tried telling them what had happened, but to no avail.

Her father rang the police when it became evident that something was wrong. The police came asking questions about her. They set up a search party and her father joined them. Beth wanted to go too and somehow show them the river, but the house would not let her leave.

She pounded against the invisible force that kept her inside. She followed the lights of the search party before, one by one, they extinguished from sight. Soft sobs, like bread crumbs, lead her into her room where her mother clutched a pillow to her chest.

Beth's heart shattered at her mother's pain. Sliding onto the bed beside her mother, she wrapped her arms around her, knowing that they would be of little comfort.

Loud voices outside sent the two women downstairs. Her father, face ashen with heartache and anguish, went to her mother and guided her to the couch. The police officer cleared his throat, glancing at her father, who nodded, before telling her mother the bad news, that her daughter's body had been found. Her mother's scream rivalled a banshee's wail as she lunged at the officer, yelling at him that he was wrong. Her father grabbed her before she reached him and they wept together.

Days, weeks, months passed with no clues as to what had happened to Beth. The police concluded it was an accident. Her parents never believed that. Countless days they searched for information on their own, always leading to the same end; no answers and more questions. The stress of it was consuming her mother, compromising her health. And finally, the search ended.

With time, Beth learned to manipulate objects and tried in any way she could to remind her parents she was alive in a different way. Her efforts seemed to scare them and soon they moved. She tried to go with them, but the house was her prison.

Only on the anniversary of her death, Valentine's Day, when the uncontrollable pull brought her to the river's edge, did she see beyond the walls of her prison. For that night, she walked along the frozen banks of the river near the place of her death.

Once, every so often, people would see her. She heard whispers of her new name through the trees: the

Red Lady. Couples catching sight of her ghostly form were in danger of sharing the same fate as herself, if they were unworthy or meant harm to their lover. She would keep the innocent ones safe. With every life she took, she prayed for the hazel-eyed boy to return to the river. With every life she saved, she begged and pleaded for peace.

Returning to the mirror, Beth gazed again at her youthful and innocent features one last time before feeling the familiar pull to the river. Her body had barely materialized when a man, weakened with age, dropped a single red rose into the river. She could already feel his guilt.

She swayed slightly to the left, catching his eye. Hazel eyes, dim with age, met hers filling her heart with recognition. Those same eyes that had haunted her for so long, turned to fear. A smile curled her red lips.

Peace at last, she thought as she stalked towards him.

AUTUMN DAYS

By Ken Orich

Circling high above the Redcoat Trail
A Red-tailed Hawk surfs the wind.
Framed by Cottonwood yellow leaves
Against blue sky that only autumn can bring.

Coulees are changing colour daily,
To soft velvet shades of brown.
Spiked by reds, oranges and yellows;
Sharp in sunlight, muted by cloud.

Branches sagging with berries ripe.
Chokecherries in purple sheen.
Rose hips and Buffalo berries red and ready
For birds on their long journey south.

Warblers, sparrows, thrushes and gulls.
Sandpipers, shorebirds, ducks and swans.
Geese overhead flying in a long Vee,
Leaving their breeding grounds up north.

Clouds turning grey and cold.
A hint of frost chills the air.
Rain drops turn to snow flakes
That melt on still warm ground.

Winter's promise is short-lived
By Indian summer in a tug-of-war
Of crisp, frosty mornings
And warm, lazy afternoons.

Chinook Arch in the west
Anchored above the Rockies.
Pumpkin-coloured sunsets,
Streaked by strawberries, lemons and grapes.

Leaves have turned to golden glow
And fall like rain on slightest breeze.

Wind sweeping them in drifts of gold
Under autumn's blustery breath.

Tree branches are naked now.
Stark grey against darkening skies;
Bending under northern winds,
Accepting winter's beckoning call.

Soon to be dressed in robes of white,
Snow glistening under late fall sun.
Until Chinook wind melts them free,
Autumn hangs on for another day.

Wreaking Havoc

By Sarah Deverall

"DA WHEELS ON the bus go 'wound and 'wound, 'wound and 'wound, 'wound and 'wound. Da wheels on the bus go 'wound and 'wound..." I shouted out the words as Momma sang them, loudly and slightly off-key.

Daddy groaned, rolling his eyes, before punching the eject button on the cassette player stopping the song mid-lyric. "Can we puh-lease sing another song?"

He smiled back at me in the rear view mirror.

"How's about this one, Jenny-Bear?" He slid another tape into the machine, cranking the volume as our all-time favourite road song blared.

Now it was Momma's turn to groan as Daddy and I shouted, "Dead skunks in da middle of da woad. Dere's a dead skunk in da middle of da woad. Dead skunk in da middle of da woad, shtinking to High Heaven!"

I grinned my gap-toothed grin, my hand grasping a soggy Cheezie. My feet beat against the edge of my car-seat, in time to the music. I had great rhythm at the age of four. I loved road trips, especially those ending at Grandma and Grandpa's house. The ones to the Hospital where the Mean Ol' Doctors looked at pictures of my brain, not so much… but since the hospital was in the same city as Grandma and Grandpa's… oh well.

We pulled to a stop at a highway intersection. Daddy turned down the volume so he could concentrate on traffic. With no audio stimulation, I resorted to staring out the window at the cars and trucks. I loved the big trucks. The one next to us was big and red, with huge black wheels and a long trailer full of logs - big logs, skinny logs - all headed for the sawmill.

I grinned at the little man in the bright green jacket, sitting atop those logs. He caught me watching him, winked mischievously and waved. I waved back.

"Who're you waving at, Jenny-Bear?" Daddy turned to stare at me from between the seats.

"Him." I pointed to the logging truck now moving forward. Daddy turned back to his driving, increasing his speed to that of the surrounding vehicles.

"Him who?" he inquired, brows furrowed as he glanced left and right.

"Da man on da twuck." I lisped, giggling as the man jumped up to dance a jig, deftly hopping from one foot to the other, waving his hands in the air. I waved again.

"I don't see any man." Daddy glanced back at me before giving Momma a quizzical look. "Do you know what she saw, Honey?" A car horn behind us honked and Daddy turned back to focus on his driving, a frown marred his usually cheerful demeanour.

"It's just her active imagination, Dear." Momma patted his arm. She turned to smile at me. "What did he look like, Sweetie?"

I pointed an orange stained finger at the truck, now pulling ahead. "Gween, on da twee."

Momma followed my direction, nodding. "Oh yes, I see him now." She smiled indulgently at me, handing me another Cheezie. "What's he doing now, Jenny?"

I strained against my restraints, craning my neck to see further down the road. "He'th thitting on da wogs, by da belts. Ooooh! Shiny!" My eyes widened at the flash of silver as the little man waved a blade in the air with a flourish.

Momma frowned as she tried to picture what I was seeing. "What's shiny, Dear?"

"He hath a knife, Momma." I scrunched my face in displeasure. "Hith Momma neber told him not to pway wif knifes."

I continued watching as the figure on the truck sliced a strap holding the logs in place. He then hopped up to move to the next one.

"He'th cutting da lellow."

Momma shook her head, turning back to face the front.

"What an imaginative girl you are, Jenny." She looked up at the truck ahead a gasped. She grabbed Daddy's arm causing the car to swerve.

"Whoa! What was that for?" He regained control of the car.

"The s….s….strap! The s...s...strap on the truck." She stuttered. "The strap came loose!" The volume of her statement increased with each word as she watched the load on the logging truck shift.

Daddy stared at the yellow strap on the truck,

now flapping wildly. He honked his horn, trying to get the driver's attention, to no avail. Momma turned wide eyes towards me, her brows wrinkled and sweat beading on her forehead. "The man on the truck. Did you see him cut the strap?"

I nodded, frowning at the serious tone of her words. *Did I do something wrong? Should I not have spoken?*

She whirled back in her seat. "Speed up, John. SPEED UP NOW!" Her foot pressed down on the floor boards as if she were the one with the gas pedal. The car pulled forward as I observed the second strap separate from the truck. The load shifted, logs bounced on the flat deck of the trailer with the movement of the truck.

Daddy rolled down his window, honking his horn, waving his arm and shouting in an attempt to get the driver's attention. But the big rig kept moving on. The passing lane was ending; Daddy had no choice but to speed past the truck.

He pulled out in front of the semi then slowed down, forcing the traffic behind him to reduce the speed. The loud blare from the truck answered his tactic.

Sweat beaded on Daddy's grimacing face, teeth clenching, knuckles white on the steering wheel.

Momma's hands flattened against the dash. I covered my ears from the noise – the loud honking, the squealing of air brakes, the grinding of gears. Then the rumble of logs, the crunch of metal, the screams....

Daddy stopped the car. He and Momma ran back to help those behind us, leaving me stuck in my car seat, held captive by the belts.

The little man in the green jacket appeared beside me, rage and hatred roiling in his eyes. "This isn't the end, Little One," he hissed at me. "I am Havoc and WE *will* meet again." He smiled menacingly before vanishing in a poof of sulfur smoke.

Forever burned into my brain – that first introduction to Havoc. It changed me. It changed my family, my relationship to my parents, my siblings and even my dog. It changed how I saw life: *Was I seeing what everyone else saw? Or was I seeing beyond the veil?*

I became the Protectress, seeking out and removing the evil from this world. Forever fighting; forever alone.

CHIPS

By Brock Sansome

"DAMN KIDS! TRESSPASSING!" The old man muttered under his breath as he shuffled along his path. It wasn't often when someone came onto his land, but when they did, it made him angry. He thought about going to his house and getting his shovel. Would someone miss the kids? No one missed the last ones.

He thought against it and pulled his cat in closer to his chest. He cuddled it tighter. "No, we won't do that to them will we? Not this time. We should follow them, shouldn't we Jeffrey? See where they go?"

The old man with bruises and cuts stepped from the path, slipping silently into the foliage of the forest. From the thickness and shadows he was able to stalk a deer. Two loud and unsuspecting boys wouldn't be a problem. He stroked his black cat on the head and nuzzled it close to his face and kissed it on the nose.

"They won't know we are there, no one ever does." His smile, broken with missing teeth spread across his face. He didn't really speak, everything he *said* was in his mind. His real voice was hoarse, unused and raspy. The only time he used it was when he cursed or yelled.

One of the boys said something, the other laughed. They hacked at the forest, cutting limbs and saplings, moving the foliage out of their way instead of being respectful and moving around it. He knew where they headed. Not his house, but his storage, where he kept his offerings.

"What do they want there?" He looked at his cat who just hung in his arms, peaceful as if dreaming or basking in the warm afternoon sun.

Through the bushes he watched them approach the shed. "I wouldn't go in there." He thought-whispered to his cat. After several moments he set his cat down beneath a bush. He thought he heard it purr and so stroked it on the top of its head. "I'll be back soon."

Carefully he approached the shed and listened to the boys speaking.

"....We don't have anything else to eat."

"What are you doing here?" This time, he spoke, his voice raspy and dry. It hurt his throat. The boys both held one of his jars, and, and were eating from them! The old man started to laugh, cackle in a high pitched roll.

"Eating? I wouldn't be eating that. Is it tasty?" It hurt his throat to speak, but he smiled, knowing it was worth it.

He laughed again as the boys shuffled, unsure of what to do. The old man bent over and scratched his leg. One boy put a jar back onto the shelf. Again, he scratched his leg. This time a scab fell away.

The old man left the shed shortly after the boys ran out, cackling and laughing to himself. "They were eating them!" He said to his cat, still huddled under the bush where he left it. Carefully picking it up again, he brought it to his nose and kissed it, letting the maggots fall away from its body and to the forest floor.

WINTER

Holidays and Hibernation

DONNER'S BLOG

By Charles James

Jan 1

SANTA THOUGHT IT would be a good idea for us to keep a blog about our experiences on the team. He said it would be good for morale, that it would help with recruitment.

I think he's losing it.

He knows we've got hooves right? You try mashing a giant toenail into a keyboard. *Zdfcsg!*

It looks like I drew the short straw on this one.

I've been trying to think of a good title for the blog – something catchy – a kind of candid, tell-all, behind-the-scenes look at what life is really like for the reindeer on Santa's team.

Blitz thought I should call it *Reindeer Leaks.*

I don't think that's such a good idea.

Where Blitz goes, nothin' grows.

It's best we don't remind people of that.

Jan 19

I'm sorry to say there's no 'Rudolph' on the team. He was made up by some department store in the thirties. Gene Autry sang a song about him. Now people think there's this cute little flashlight-faced reindeer up front leading the team. You know what you see when you turn on your high-beams in a snow storm?

Snow!

We've had radar on the sled since 1961, so it's not like we really need a light up front. And we do have a Ferdinand… Ferdinand the Taillight Reindeer. He runs behind the sleigh.

Jan 28

The team breaks down like this.

Up front you've got your *lead deer*, Dash and Dance. These guys steer the team and set the pace. They're like the fighter pilots of reindeer. They can see everything without a tail in the face. They're the ones the kids will run up to and pet. They smile for the camera. But really, leading is just pointing everyone else in a direction.

Next you've got your *swing deer*, Prance and Vix. They swing the rest of the team behind them in turns or curves on the trail. Swinging takes a lot of skill. You swing wrong through a turn and it throws everyone else off pace. In a worst case scenario, you flip the sled.

The next guys are the *team deer*, that's Dave and Irving. They add power to the team. Usually that's where we put the rookies… not too much responsibility to start out with.

Finally you come to the anchors, me and Blitz. We're called *wheel deer*. We take the brunt of the sleigh's weight. So if you're ever looking for ideas for what to ask Santa for, here's some: feathers, balloons, helium, happy thoughts.

I mean Jeez, some people give each other houses for Christmas. *Houses!* Seriously?

Feb 14

Vix is the only doe on the team right now. If you ever see us out on a Christmas run, you'll know her because she's the only one with antlers. Bucks lose their antlers in the fall, does keep them year round.

I'll admit I've got a crush on Vix.

You shouldn't fall for someone on your team. If it doesn't work out then things will be all awkward. But you can't help who you fall for, right?

You'd think I could just ask her out, but every time she comes close it's like I've got hooves in my mouth.

Feb 21

Okay, so like Blitz has Ferdinand convinced he's turning into a caribou.

The whole team's in on it. Maybe it ain't common knowledge among humans, but reindeer ARE caribou.

For all the deersplaining Ferdinand does, he ain't exactly the quickest deer in the woods.

He came out to the pasture the other day, and he was all worried that his antlers were lopsided. Dash looks at him kind of funny and says, "Are you sure you're not turning into a caribou?"

Ferdinand goes, "What? A caribou? Oh. No."

Without missing a beat, Prance comes in. "Dude, you're really looking off." He cocks his head to the side. "You totally look like a caribou. You sure you're feeling okay?"

"Yeah. Fine."

"Oh. Good," says Prance. "Cause if you were a caribou your antlers would get all velvety and stuff."

Dude's been checking out his reflection by the ice pond for the last three days.

Mar 10

The Ghosts of Christmas Past, Present and Future all showed up at the North Pole this week.

It was tense.

Apr 17

Christmas Eve, the Big Guy gets the milk and cookies. *Maybe* we get a carrot.

All the way around the world in a single night and the best you can do is a fricken' carrot?

Reindeer don't even eat carrots. We eat lichen, grass, and leaves.

No carrots.

May 9

I woke up about two o'clock in the morning. A blinding red light like a giant laser was beaming into the stables. And it wasn't constant either. It would beam on and then die off. The stable was nearly black and then just as I'd get back to sleep, BLAM, there is was again.

So I head outside and follow it up the road to the northern end of Christmas Town.

And there's Ferdinand with his tongue on the North Pole calling out, "Tuck! Tuck! Ma tongue ith tuck!"

Underneath a snowshoe hair has his feet up against the pole and was pushing on Ferdinand's chest. Behind him is a snowman yanking on Ferdinand's hips. And they're all organized about it. "One. Two. Three. Heave!" Ferd's tongue stretches out about a foot and then his tail ignites.

You ever see one of those fibre-optic lamps, the kind you can run your fingers over with little lights coming out the end? His tail's kind of like that. Each time his tongue stretched out the lights would go from a soft white to a laser intense red.

"Ferdinand, how'd your tongue get stuck?" I asked.

"Pranther triple deer dared me."

June 17

Not many people know we crashed the sled last

year.

Sorry if anyone's presents were wet, by the way.

It all started when we were out on our run and all of a sudden Twinkle Tail is hungry. And everywhere is closed, because, guess what… it's Christmas Eve. You know what's open at three in the morning on Christmas Eve?

Taco Time.

We pulled up to the drive through and Ferdinand orders like a dozen Chili Burritos. Prance figured he was buying for the team, but then right in front of us he wolfs the whole dozen down, just like that. Then he looks up, belches a wet one, and says, "Aren't you guys getting anything?"

We were ahead of schedule. All of a sudden the Big Guy has another one of his ideas. He asks Ferdinand if he wants to run up front for a bit. We're all quietly shaking our heads, trying to pass the hint to Old Claus that putting Ferdinand up front ain't a great idea, but he insists… in the spirit of Christmas or something.

About half an hour later we're over Medicine Hat and Prance looks back and he's like, "You guys smell something?"

We all start poking our noses up in the air, like we want to smell it. Anyway, it took a minute, but then I caught a whiff.

It was melt-your-eyeballs bad. Like I was in tears. The swing deer go left instead of right and the sleigh starts spiraling out of control. Santa turns as green as an elf and blows chunks all over the front seat.

I've got tears in my eyes and the sky is all blurry. I've got no idea where I'm going. When I do blink the tears away, there's Ferdinand, la-dee-da, la-dee-da, check out my freakin' tail. And he's got his phone out texting.

Next thing I know Dave's ass is in my face.

WHAM! We hit the ground hard.

Santa crawls out of the sleigh and makes a B-line for the Shell station, a white glove over his mouth.

Ferdinand doesn't have a scratch on him. He looks up from his phone and says, "Hey guys, check it out. The elves liked my selfie over the Eiffel Tower."

<u>July 21</u>

That was a pretty monumental wipeout last year, but amazingly no one was hurt. Just as we were about to pulverize Old Beacon Bottom, Blitz pipes up. "Uh.

Guys?" He points to the ground.

An old woman lay on the ground, hoof marks all over her body.

"I don't think she's breathing," Irving says.

"Oh come on." I lean down, give her a nudge. Nothing. Her skin's already cold.

"What do we do?" Prance asks. "Guys. We could go to prison for this. I can't go to prison. They only give you like one pair of underwear a week in prison."

"That's what you're worried about right now?" Blitz says. "Reindeer don't even wear underwear."

Prance thinks for a second and says. "But if we did that would be, like really unhygienic."

"Focus team," Vixen says. "Santa's coming back."

"Don't worry. It's all taken care of," says Ferdinand.

We all look down and the body's… gone. There's a giant red streak in the snow, but that's it. The body just disappeared.

"Ferdinand, where's the old woman?" I ask.

"Don't worry. No one's going to find her."

"Ho. Ho. Ho." Big Red was a little less jolly, but he'd managed to get most of the puke out of his beard.

We all stand in front of the red stain. Nothing to see here.

"On we go," Vix says. We all subtly kick snow over the blood with our back hooves.

Just like that, we go back to work.

Aug 25

Okay. I'm going to ask Vix out.

She's single. I'm single.

I'll just walk up to her and say "Hi." It's all about being natural, being confident, right?

Wish me luck.

Aug 26

Kill me now.

Ferdinand asked Vix out like right in front of me. I was playing it cool, kicking some snow. And he prances up, flashes that tail and he's all like "Hey what are you doing Friday?"

And she's all like, "Nothing."

And he goes, "I got tickets to the Narwhal concert. You wanna come?"

And she's like, "Yeah, sure."

Man, Ferdinand gets all the tail.

Sept 16

A few people have written into the blog wondering what happened to that woman we ran over.

Well, we made the last few houses without saying much of anything and then the run was done. All the elves wanted to celebrate, but all the deer just wanted to go back to the stables. On the way back I had to ask. I go up to Ferdinand and whisper, "So where is she?"

Ferdinand turns back and shrugs. "I hid her."

"How?"

"DUH. We had a sleigh full of wrapping paper. I wrapped her up."

"You wrapped up a dead body? In giftwrap?"

"I used the red paper… with sparkles. No need to thank me,"

"Ferd," says Vix. "You can't do that. Someone's going to miss her. We have to get her back to her family."

Ferdinand thinks about it for a moment. "I suppose you're right."

"So where is she?"

"I put her in the sack, with all the other presents. That way no one would find her."

Blitz starts looking through the bag, but it's

empty. "She's not here. Ferdinand, how far down did you stuff her?"

Twinkle Tail thinks about it for a moment. "I don't know. I guess she would have come out somewhere in Mexico."

Oct 20

Vix and Ferdinand didn't work out!

I can't say I'm surprised. That guy thinks he's the king of the forest.

So she's back on the market.

How long do you wait to ask out someone who's just single anyway? I mean, I don't want to be the rebound deer. But I gotta put it out on the table, don't I?

Nov 4

Time trials today.

Each deer has to loop down to the South Pole and make it back within an hour – all staying in the same time zone.

No problem.

Nov 17

Well we found out what happened to that woman we ran over.

By Christmas morning, we're all turning in to the stable. Blitz flips on the TV though. He never misses the Queen's Christmas Message.

"Guys? It looks like we found her."

The entire team crowded around Blitz's TV. It turned out that under the mistletoe in Puerto Vallarta, some family strung up a rather macabre piñata. No one noticed it was a little old lady until after about an hour of beating it with the Christmas piñata stick.

Ferdinand's tail lights up. "Well, it looks like everyone's a winner this Chrismas." Then he trots off to bed.

<u>Dec 23</u>

Big night tomorrow night.

I'm feeling loose.

Dave says he has a sprained hoof. He slipped on some ice yesterday and the guy's been limping around… "oh, my hoof, my hoof."

The thing is it switches sides.

Anyway, now we gotta call up a kid from the minors.

The Big Guy was talking about someone who

calls himself Powerball.

Must be a friend of Ferdinand's.

Dec 26

Okay, normally I'd be asleep right now. Normally I sleep through the New Year, but I gotta tell someone.

So we get back from the run and there's no mishaps this year. Not one. Powerball did a good job. Ferdinand didn't get stuck in anything. But as we're cleaning up, Vix has got her head in the sleigh and she's like, "Hey there's a present left in here."

There's always something.

I come over and take a look, and I ain't seein' nothing, but a sleigh floor.

I look up and she smiles and kisses me!

I'm in love.

HER LAST GIFT

By Shannon Still (L.K. Winters)

I STARED AT the blinking black line. It was worse than a strobe light. For hours I stared at its hypnotic pulse in the hopes my muse would strike. But absolutely no inspiration came. Muse, why do you hate me so? Was it really fair to blame the muse as my hindrance for my lack of writing? Or maybe I couldn't write at all.

The new page remained mockingly blank and an assignment was due in less than twelve hours. Still nothing! My fingers couldn't even connect with the keys to type anything, which told me how bad it was. I cradled my face in my hands, my elbows braced on the desk. Why won't my imagination work?

"Ahhhh!!!" I pushed my rolling chair away in frustration. Away from the offending computer that I couldn't biblically "pluck out" for offending me so. The push was a little rougher than I intended and I braced for impact. My shoulder clenched, resolved to the fact of future pain.

A sudden stop rescued my shoulder from a bruising impact but didn't rescue my bottom from a jarring encounter with the floor.

"Ow!" I tilted sideways to rub my backside when a not so successful suppressed deep laugh came from the door. I glanced up through squinted eyelids.

"Jeremy! What the H!" I tried to sound angry at my boyfriend, but then I looked into his handsome features. His bright smile and warm laugh calmed my anger, nudging me to laugh at the situation too.

"Sorry, Shan." He pushed the chair out of the way with his foot then bent to help me up. As he bent, a tendril of black hair touched the corner of his blue eyes. I couldn't stop looking into them as his strong arms lifted me. They sure didn't need any assistance from my weak limbs.

"I only meant to stop you from crashing against the wall. I guess the floor had other plans for you." His laughter, now unsuppressed, filled my apartment.

Once up, my back toward the computer, I wrapped my arms around Jeremy, leaning against his chest with my ear planted over his heart. He laid his stubbled chin on my unwashed, dark brown hair. I'd been so preoccupied all day, watching the blinking black line and waiting for the muse, that showering had been shoved down to the bottom of the list of priorities. But Jeremy didn't seem to care. Or maybe he did, but chose not to say anything, which always earned him good graces.

Thump tha-thump tha-thump. My breathing slowed to the lullaby of his heartbeat. I closed my eyes ready to fall asleep in his arms.

"Shan, you haven't written anything," he said against my ear. A point of fact I already knew. I let it slide because the sound of his voice was so peaceful. I pulled away with only a slight gap between us, his arms still around me, to look back at the computer.

"I... I can't... It's just not in me anymore. I can't find the ideas, the words, the inspiration, the imagination. Whatever you want to call it, I can't find it. It's like it's been blocked off by a big, gigantic wall or something. It's not there anymore."

I pressed myself back into his arms wanting to

drift off to sleep and forget the assignment, the world, the emotions, just for a little while.

"I see a connection," he whispered in my hair.

I glimpsed up as he looked down.

"You do?" When I couldn't see, I knew he could. That's why I loved him.

"I know what today is. You know this started when..." His words trailed off.

Now I knew what connection he was making, for my lack of creativity.

"Please, Jeremy, don't say it," I begged, leaving the security of his arms to go sit on my chair. He followed suit and knelt in front of me, taking my hands.

"Alright, I won't, if you promise to do something in exchange." Those blue eyes peered into mine, challenging me.

"Fine, what is it you want me to do?" I let out a breath shaking my head. I easily caved, I would do anything for him.

"You need to go see *HIM.*"

I shook my head. I would do anything except that. That the idea even entered his mind baffled me.

"I ca...." I was about to refuse when Jeremy pressed his lips to mine. "Mm."

"You promised," he whispered against my lips.

"I did," I sighed in agreement, running my hand down his cheek then kissing him again. "What do I have to do?"

"All you have to do," he pulled out his wallet from his back pocket, removing a fifty and handing it to me. "Is take this money."

I took it, placing it in my jeans pocket.

"Now you need an item that has sentimental value from her," he said.

I placed my hand over the rose stone angel necklace Jo had given me a year ago. A guardian angel for her guardian angel.

"Last, but not least, an item that belongs to you, something that you bought or made." Hmmm. I scanned the office. My eye caught a sparkling, purple butterfly bracelet pinned above the computer. I had made it when I was a little girl with mother before she became sick. I reached up and slowly took it off the pin.

"Okay, all set. I just have to shower." I started for the bathroom, but he grabbed me before I got out the door.

"No time for a shower, Shan, you need to go now." He sounded like it was a matter of life and death.

"But Jeremy, I am beginning to stink and I swear I saw black mold growing between my toes." I laughed but one look at his serious face made me stop. "Okay, I'll go now. Where do I go?" I placed my items in my leather handbag.

Through the years I had lost track of where Mark lived. It was hard to keep track of him, he moved so many times, though his phone number always stayed the same.

"The Old Bridge Road towards Driftwood Lake," he said, then kissed me, swatting my bottom as I exited.

THE OLD BRIDGE Road lived up to its name of Old. I am not sure how often it got used, if ever. With each bump my rusty Chevy and I hit, my insides heavily cursed Jeremy, who insisted on staying behind, saying I needed to do this alone. Somehow, my Chevy and I made it intact.

It was 8:30 PM when I pulled up in front of *HIS* cabin, made from the same driftwood resting along the shore. The water sparkled with tiny diamonds that didn't break when the little waves hit the stilts holding up the cabin protruding out over the lake.

I got out of my car, automatically locking it. The sound seemed out of place in this quiet solitude, only broken by the sound of the rushing river flowing into the lake.

"Sunshine! You came!" Mark appeared, stopping halfway down the stairs. My step-dad was a true hippie if there ever was one. Long blond hair tied back in ponytail with a white bandana covering his forehead. An equally blond beard hung past his collarbone nestled within the vee of his pink flowered shirt, which was tucked into his blue jean bell bottoms. The usual love and peace jewellery hung around his neck.

"Hello, Mark," I said, reluctantly walking toward the wooden stairs, pausing at the first step. I wanted to turn around. This was ridiculous. What was I doing here? I didn't believe his insane ideologies. Before I could turn tail and run, he took my arm

"No time for pleasantries or reminiscing! The time is nearly upon us," he said urgently excited. The only thing that wasn't true hippie about him was the way he spoke. It was more like an English gentleman.

Time? What time? That got my feet moving up the stairs and I followed him into his lavender-incensed home, nearly choking on the fumes. Mark motioned for me to sit in a cushion on an extremely orange shag carpet, which I didn't do.

"Did you bring the items and the fifty I won from Jeremy in a bet?" he asked.

I handed him the fifty from my back pocket and the objects that were stashed in my handbag, making a mental note to ask Jeremy about a certain bet.

"Good, good." He took the two objects then began to search for something in his drawers and cupboards while I inspected his home.

There wasn't much in the way of electricity. The light that entered the home through the windows pierced the clouds of incense smoke. Candles and lamps were set in various places around the room. A wood burning stove sat neatly in the corner. There were doors leading off to different parts of the cabin, all made from the same driftwood as the outside of the cabin.

Mark kept searching for whatever it was as I continued looking around the room. Shelves of different lengths held various religious objects from the Virgin

Mary to Buddha. Framed pictures on the walls showed different buildings like an Aztec temple and a strange looking building that was a cross between a Greek and Aztec design; below it was written Cardston, Alberta Temple. What religion was that? I didn't get any further with that question when a loud bang brought me back.

"Found it!"

'It' looked like a piece of chalk. He wrapped the angel necklace and butterfly bracelet at each end of the chalk then handed it to me.

I didn't take it. "What is that for?"

"I want you to draw a door, on the door. Make sure the handle is on the inside of the door you draw," he said, with no hesitation about how strange it sounded.

"Draw a door on the door? And how is this going to help me?" I was very sceptical at this point. Nope, that was a lie, I was sceptical when Jeremy first mentioned it.

"The spirit world and our world are very closely connected. There are certain areas in the world that will allow a person to travel to the spirit world for a short time."

"What areas? Is this cabin built on such an area?"

"Not built on, but beside. The river flows into the

lake. This cabin is built facing the flowing river and the door is exactly parallel to the mouth of the river, where it meets the lake."

"So, all these spiritual spots are on rivers?"

"They don't have to be. They can face west, east or north. Never south or one might…never mind, the thought is too horrible to imagine. To open the door the sun has to be behind, which can be difficult, depending when the earth rotates. Even one-way streets can be used. It can be quite aggravating though; when someone drives down in the opposite way it was intended, it messes with the balance. It takes a long time to get back."

I did remember him at one time living on a one-way street and being very particular about the architecture of the house.

"Hurry, time is running out." He pushed the chalk toward me again and this time I took it.

"What is this made out of? And why are my things around it?"

"The chalk is made out of bones of the Saints, dirt from a widow's grave, and holy water."

I fumbled with the chalk nearly dropping it.

"I am joking, of course, it is just normal chalk,"

he said. "The items though hold significance. The one that she has given you will summon her to you in the spirit world. The other will allow you to return back to the real world."

"Why are you worried about time?"

"The closer to the time a person has departed this life, the stronger the energies between this world and the next are, allowing for an easier entrance. Not that it can't be done any other day, I just found the success rate better on the day and time they have passed. Make sure you draw the door on this side with the angel end and the way back with the butterfly end."

I had no more questions so I did as he asked. Making sure the angel end was up, I drew the door with the handle of the real door within mine.

"Now pull it open, walk through and find who you seek. When you are ready to return draw another door and pull."

I placed my hand on handle as the clock struck nine, the exact time that she had passed away.

"Mark, it will just show me the outside of the cabin and I will break your door opening it that way," I said as my hand began to turn the handle. My spirit seemed to know what my mind didn't.

"Have a little faith. Open the door," he whispered and I did.

I almost fell on my bottom again.

It wasn't the outside of the cabin I saw, with my car parked outside, but a darkened eastern sky and a brilliant yellow horizon in the west. Between the two horizons lay golden candles of wheat swaying in the wind.

I looked back at Mark, scared and hesitant to walk through. He motioned me with his hands to take the step. I looked forward then walked through, the door shutting behind me.

I stood on a long-railed porch that disappeared around the corners of the house with stairs situated below the door. Two rocking chairs sat on the left.

I placed the chalk in my pocket before sitting in one and began to rock. This was the white farmhouse where we were supposed to grow old together after our husbands died. I held back the tears that threatened to fall, then I heard her voice like the angel she was.

"What's up, ShanShan?" Always her greeting, my sister, my friend, Jo.

There she sat in the rocking chair next to mine

keeping in perfect time with me. Her black hair, with the raspberry pink underneath, was thick and full, no longer falling out and thin. Her cheeks and eyes were not sunken, but rosy and bright.

Tears fell down my cheeks. Her appearance may have changed while she was sick during those two years but never her heart.

"I have been missing you," I blurted out. I didn't know how long I had. I didn't look away. "It's nine months today since you passed away."

She held out her hand and I took it. It was as warm as freshly baked bread.

"I am having a hard time with you gone," I continued, blinking back tears. "I know that my grief is not the same as others, because I wasn't biologically related to you, but I hurt immensely just the same. My heart ripped into two and a large piece was taken the moment I was told you died."

"I miss you too, more than you know," she said, giving me a sad smile. "I'm not really gone, ShanShan, you just can't see me all the time. But I know you feel me. I talk to you when you need help. I sit with you in your car when you are having a bad day, and I get to share the good times with you."

I kept crying as Jo continued.

"You have every reason to feel sorrow. We are more than just friends, we are best friend, sisters in soul, and nothing will ever tear that apart. Not even death."

She set her hand on my shoulder.

"Speaking of tearing apart, you need to break down that wall and let everything flow back in, Honey." Jo raised her eyebrow as she often did when she was being serious in a loving way. "It's not good to live that way. You need to live, ShanShan."

"I keep expecting you to be at your house waiting for me to come over so that we can make plans for our futures. But you aren't."

"Nope, I'm not. You need to let that go, Shan-Shan. I am not waiting for you there but I am waiting for you here. It won't be too long before we can be together again."

We sat there holding hands, talking about different topics, laughing and crying for what seemed an eternity. I glanced down at my skin. It began to grow old with spots, wrinkling and thinning as did hers. Our hands never let go of each other. Though I could not see mine, her face gracefully aged as I hoped mine did. Her last gift to me, a fulfilling of a dream, until we would meet again.

An overwhelming pull brought me out of the rocking chair.

Jo stood up too and we hugged each other tight. I didn't want to let go but the invisible pull drew me away to face the door and I took out the chalk. With the butterfly end, I drew a door on the old white farmhouse door, handle inside it. Then, I turned its warm steel surface and pushed.

I looked back. Jo was still standing there with a big 'you will be alright' smile and a single white tear falling down her cheek.

"I love you, ShanShan," she said. Then, she was gone.

"I love you too," I whispered through tears.

I stepped through the door and the wall around my heart began to crumble.

REINDEER GAMES

By Bianca Rowena

"ATTENTION EVERYONE!" CAPTAIN Jordan T. Clark, whose real name was Bill and who actually worked at a car dealership on the outskirts of town, cleared his throat and addressed the motley crew of Star Trek enthusiasts gathered at the Loyal Order of Goose Hall. "I'd like to call to order the Starship U.S.S. King Edward's Fifth Annual Winter Solstice Festival on this--"

"Sir?"

"What is it, Ensign?"

"I thought this was a Christmas party."

Ensign Rudy (which was short for Rudolf, a German name meaning Famous Wolf), was dressed in a particularly hideous Christmas sweater and had brought gifts for everyone in the group. Whether or not he was disappointed that no one had brought him a gift in return was not evident to Bill. Nothing grated on his nerves more than a new member who didn't know how to role play, or didn't stay in character during their meetings.

Bill sighed. "That may be what the humans called their celebrations on Earth, before the Sixth World War, but in this century, and for the sake of all those present," Bill glanced around the room at the green, blue and brown faces, "we are simply calling our celebration the Winter Solstice. Rok Khan," Bill turned to the burly man to his right, "tell us about the Klingon Winter Solstice celebrations."

Rok Khan nodded and puffed up his chest. He was a beefy middle aged man with waist length hair who worked at the bottle depot downtown and never moved past the 80's-metal hair band era. He sat up straighter in his Klingon battle uniform. Bill loved Rok Khan. No one knew his real name. It didn't matter. He was so dedicated to their role playing he never went out of character.

"Ram nI'tay," Rok Khan started, "which is our Winter Solstice festival, originated from a community need to share resources during the leanest hunting season." Rok Khan's stony expression never wavered.

"Understandable," Bill said. "Thank you, Rok Khan. T'Prel, what about the Vulcans?"

Tamara, aka T'Prel, the resident Vulcan, was an amazing actress, having graduated from the London School of Dramatic Arts and yet somehow ended up here, in small town Alberta, her beauty and talent left painfully undiscovered.

Bill had long ago given up on pursuing her as a romantic prospect, after the summer BBQ, when she almost broke his hand after he tried to put his arm around her while yawning.

She looked at him now, with a distinctly Vulcan expression on her face; a calculated mixture of boredom and condescending indifference to those around her.

"Vulcans do not partake in such celebrations. During the winter solstice we spend four hours in meditation reflecting on the inner darkness of our souls while simultaneously recommitting ourselves to the suppression of our emotions, which may try to surface during the winter months on Vulcan, a season in which we are forced to spend extended periods of time indoors and in close quarters with..." T'Prel's patronizing glare scanned the room, "... others."

"Thank you, T'Prel, now-"

"Um… Captain? Sir?" Ensign Rudy raised his hand again, making Bill feel like a high school teacher, rather than the Captain of a Federation Starship.

Bill rubbed at his eyes. "What is it now, Ensign?"

"About the reindeer games, will we be taking turns on the computers?"

A shiver travelled down Bill's spine at the thought of Ensign Rudy's grubby fingers on his customized Alienware gaming laptop, which cost him more than his car did. "There aren't enough computers for everyone to pilot a starship on this mission, for the Winter Solstice games," he said. Why didn't Rudy just get his own damn computer already? "Maybe you can co-pilot with Rok Khan on his computer?"

Rok Khan grunted. The others all shifted uncomfortably in their seats. Bill looked around the room. Everyone avoided his eyes. Well, it wasn't his problem.

"Alright everyone, let's get our laptops situated."

The room filled with excited chatter and movement as everyone pulled out their laptops, all but Ensign Rudy, who remained in his seat. He looked left and right, as though trying to decide who the weakest member of the fleet was, so he could convince them to let him play on their laptop. He couldn't seem to find a single one.

The Starship U.S.S. King Edward crew may have been a strange lot, but they were definitely not prone to pity. Not Klingons or Vulcans or Romulans, definitely not Andorians. As for Bill, being a human male captain, he prided himself in his ability to remain logical and not easily swayed by dangerous emotions such as pity. These emotions could impact his decision-making as the Captain of a Starship, potentially making the difference between life and death for the entire crew!

"Let the Reindeer Games begin!" Bill announced moments later, when everyone was logged onto the multi-player game.

Soon the games were underway and all thoughts of Ensign Rudy dissipated as the room erupted with shouts of battle, mostly coming from Rok Khan.

Suddenly the front door of the Goose Lodge flew open, startling everyone, and in stepped the sexiest looking female that Captain Bill had ever laid eyes on. He heard the sound of his starship crashing into an asteroid on his computer screen. There were other such sounds coming from the other laptops around the room as more starships crashed and everyone's eyes turned to the sight before them. Even T'Prel had stopped playing, except she had logically paused her game play first.

"Is this the Samson Party?" the sexy Miss Claus cooed. Bill, as the Captain, should have spoken first, but he was dumbstruck. His eyes travelled up from the temptress's fuzzy boots, over her long, bare legs, to the tight, short red skirt with fuzzy white trim hugging her perfect thighs. Bill shivered in delight as his glance made its way to the voluptuous cleavage surrounded by white fluffy softness. He swallowed hard.

"This isn't the Samson Party," T'prel droned from somewhere behind him.

"Oh," the temptress set her hand on a curvy hip. "Well it's blizzarding out there and I can't see a thing. Does anyone know where 619, 7th Ave South is?"

"I do!" Ensign Rudy bellowed, putting up his hand. Miss Claus's glance turned to him. His cheeks and nose were flushed red and he couldn't keep his eyes above her chin.

"You," she said. "With the nose." Miss Claus pointed to Rudy's potato-like noggin. "Follow me, and take me to this place. I've got five other performances tonight and you can help me get there." She stopped, then brought her voice down an octave. "Does watching five strip teases in a row sound okay to you Red Nose?"

"Yes, Ma'am!" Rudy jumped up from his chair, knocking it over. He nodded eagerly and tripped over the chair legs on his way to Miss Claus.

"Alright," she snickered, taking in all the laptops huddled together on a table. "Sorry for interrupting your… games. I've only got room for one in the car, so I'm taking this one."

She waggled a finger seductively at Rudy, who followed her out into the blizzard, forgetting his jacket on the chair he'd tripped over in his hurry.

The front door shut and the room was quiet. After a moment the sounds of a starship racing started up from T'Prel's laptop.

"I'm winning," she said, as the rest of the group sighed in defeat.

IN THE EYE OF THE BEHOLDER

By Leslie Johnson

"WHOOPSIE DAISY! OHH! Deep breath! Deep breath. I love the roller coaster!" My googly eyes spun around making me feel a little dizzy.

"It's not a roller coaster, you idiot." Green Ball shouted down to me. "Mr. Davidson is moving us out of the garage."

"Really? Wow! That means it's almost Christmas– the most magical time of year! Whoo hoo! Oops, bumpy ride, bumpy ride. Steady as she goes, Mr. Davidson– steady now!"

"Everybody, quick! Close your eyes!" Gold Ball barked. PPOPP! The lid to our plastic tote pulled away and light streamed into our darkness. "Slowly, now. Open your eyes."

"Wow – they've painted the living room since last year. I like that colour – what would you call it? Buttered Rum?" Red Ball asked.

"I can't see anything – what is buttered rum?" I shouted from my place near the bottom of the tote. I tried to lift myself up but my popsicle stick body was too stiff.

"There's the tree." Red Ball drawled. "Gosh it's a beauty – so full and lush. Breathe deep guys – that's pine– isn't it nice? The Davidsons never go with artificial – they love the real thing."

I drew in a deep breath. Even through all the other decorations, the faint smell of pine reached me. I almost wept with joy in anticipation of hanging on the tree again.

"Would you shut up! You'd think none of us had been here before – but we have. We've all been here. We don't need the commentary." Green Ball snapped.

"Good grief, Where is your Christmas Spirit?" Gold Ball demanded. "Lighten up or you'll be at the back of the tree where no one can see and admire you."

The tote fell silent for a minute. "Look, the lights are on. Isn't that pretty?" Red Ball was back to her commentary.

"Okay, here comes Mrs. Davidson. Get ready people. It's our turn." Gold Ball smiled. "Be brave now–there's plenty of room on this tree for all of us. Away we go!"

And he was gone. Red went next, then Green. My tote companions disappeared one by one as Mrs. Davidson reached inside and pulled them out into the world and onto the tree. My stomach turned over with anticipation. Who was I going to be near this year? Which way would I face? I surely didn't want the back view again–the wall. No one could admire me if they weren't able to see me. I didn't like it back there. It was depressing, and scary.

Last year, the cat crept into the back corner regularly. She was only there to cause trouble. Several times she attempted to pull me off the tree. I screamed for help but there wasn't anyone close enough to help me. Thankfully, my string held and she didn't have her way with me. Those sharp teeth could have done major damage to my fragile form. Bad Kitty!

Most of my fellow decorations were gone. The ribbons, the shiny balls, the hobby horses. I counted six of us now, languishing on the soft bed of cotton that lines the bottom of the tote. That's when the world went dark. What the….

"Guess you're one of us now, Little Popsicle Stick Rudolf." The half walnut shell with the cotton ball beard chuckled. "You're no longer good enough to be on the tree."

I was crushed. After years of hanging in the front near the top, then moving down to the bottom and finally being hung at the back of the tree - this was my destiny? To languish in the bottom of a stupid plastic tote, waiting to be thrown out. It would be better to be discarded! At least then I wouldn't feel the pain of rejection every year. This was the worst.

We waited for the tote to be moved back to garage. Then I heard a voice. It was muffled, but familiar. I couldn't make out the words but her voice lifted my spirits. Penny! I was sure of it. She sounded more grown up than when she made me. She was only six and fifteen years had passed since then. "I'm sure that's Penny's voice," I told the others, straining hard to hear what she was saying.

"Don't know." said Walnut Santa. "I can't make out nothing."

The tote lid was unexpectedly pulled away. I was blinded and quickly shut my eyes. A soft hand scooped me up. "There you are!" said Penny, kindly. "Time to find you a new home. And you and you and you."

The six of us were slipped into a small paper sack. We were jostled and jolted for a time before the bag was reopened. Penny pulled us out and with great tenderness, she placed us on a small artificial tree. The pretend needles were more ticklish than real ones and they didn't smell very nice. But the view was terrific.

"This is fantastic!" Walnut Santa said. "I haven't been hung on a tree for years. I love this tiny room. It's quaint!"

I looked around. Yes, it was small and non-descript. The furniture was shabby and worn, but there was Penny standing next to a tall, thin man I didn't know. "See Max! They are lovely. All the little ornaments I made in elementary school. Aren't they perfect? They are just what the tree needed." She smiled as the man squeezed her closer.

"I'm glad your mother never tossed them out. They go nicely with the ones I made. Look at my Egg Carton Snowman. He looks perfect next to your Paper Plate Star."

I looked around, as far as my little googly eyes would go and hanging to my upper left was a cinnamon stick star. She winked at me! I blushed. It really was going to be a magical Christmas – after all.

A COOKIE FOR SANTA

By Sarah Deverall

IT WAS A SILENT night. The snow flakes drifted down like a scene from that Hallmark Holiday movie that played on the moving picture box on the wall. I peeked out from my perch on the third branch from the top of my tree. Yes. It was *my* tree. It was no longer in *my* forest but it was still *my* tree.

It happened three days ago. I had just returned from foraging and had settled down in my cozy nest when my world began to shake. My house would have toppled from its perch if I had not the foresight to build it among the densest of branches at the top of the tree. The next thing I knew, my world came crashing down. My winter pantry almost buried me alive. I squealed in fright at the jerky movements my tree was making.

Soon my tree was upright again. But the noise that

arose, my goodness, I had never heard the like! Such shrieking and giggling. I was sure I was about to be discovered.

I almost leapt out of my fur when a hand pushed a bauble among the branches, close to my home. Then I smelled a most delightful aroma and saw a wonderful treat being strung around my tree.

I heard the human female say it was popcorn. They must surely know I am here to leave me such an offering.

I wanted to reveal myself to the humans, to thank them, but the feral hissing and growling that came from the creature below the tree, frightened me back to my nest.

Silence fell and I crept out to the end of a branch to peep, and what should I espy in the glow of the moon-light? A platter of more treats beside a glass of white stuff, on a low table before the fireplace.

As quiet as can be, I scurried down my tree. I scampered over brightly wrapped parcels and to the table. Sniffing the air, I could not discern the scent of the dreaded beast. I leapt to the table. Flicking my bushy tail, I tiptoed to the plate of goodies. My whiskers twitched in delight at the aroma of oatmeal, raisins and nuts. I was on to a good thing here; maybe I'd stay a while.

I stretched my paw out for the treat. I almost had it within my grasp when I heard the ominous growl of t*he beast!* I raced back to the safety of my tree, jumping over parcels and up the trunk. The Beast was right behind me. I ignored the crash and tinkle as baubles bounced and broke on the hard floor. My house began to tip as the creature chased me up the tree.

"Mittens!" The shout came from across the room. "Clare! Your cat is in the tree!" The cat swore and hissed as he was yanked from my sight. I heard him and the human muttering as they left the room.

I waited a while longer, minutes... hours... I could not tell, praying the beast known as Mittens would not return. When it seemed as though he would not, I descended from my nest. I was about to make the leap from the branch to the low table to collect my treat when there came a thump and a cloud of soot billowed up from the fireplace. This was accompanied by a cough and a gruff voice muttering, "Why can't I come in through the door like a normal person?"

An exasperated voice echoed down from above,

"Because you are not a 'Normal' person."

The giant of a man in a red suit with white trim, tinged with soot, emerged from the fireplace. He stood, then smiled when he spotted the treats on the platter. He reached to take one. I leapt from my hiding spot to the table, rising to my full height of 4.35 inches, paws on my hips. How dare he take *my* treat. I gave him my fiercest scowl. But alas, he had already turned, distracted by the red sack that landed with a thud behind him.

I crept closer to the treats. The big man settled more parcels under *my* tree and I reached out to snag a cookie.

"And here is a gift for you, Wilfred." I jumped back, dropping my cookie in astonishment. *He knows my name!* I stared at the tiny parcel wrapped in shiny red paper the man set beside me.

"For me?" I squeaked.

"Yes. For you, Mr, Wilfred R. Squirrel," his bushy white eyebrows furrowed. "That is your name, is it not?" He reached out to take the parcel from my grasp. I hugged it to my chest as I nodded solemnly.

Santa smiled, sitting back in the chair next to the low table. He picked up the glass of white stuff and took a long drink. He pointed a chubby finger at me. "For you, then, Mr. Wilfred. May I have a cookie?"

I sniffled back the tears that started to form. Nobody had ever given me a gift before. I was touched. I pushed the treat into Santa's hand.

THE HEIRLOOM

By Amanda Chomiak

I WAS THERE for Becky's first Christmas. Her second and third, too. The pile of gifts for the cherished child only grew in size every year. It was safe to say the girl was spoiled rotten. Good and truly rotten.

When Anders joined the once family of three, the first boy in five generations on his mother's side, everyone was thrilled. Except young Becky.

No one saw it. Not really. Of course, they noticed the pout on her cherubic face when she realized half of the gifts beneath the tree that year had her brother's name lovingly scrawled on the label. The subtle looks of longing when Anders giggled and her parents cooed in return.

Tantrums during her fifth and sixth holiday season were not so effective. Her gradual shift to violence was missed by most, of course. A pinch to her brother's arm, a smack on his leg were easy to hide.

Joslyn and Garrick had their own problems by the girl's seventh Christmas. Drinking for Mom, a torrid affair for Dad. No one knew, of course. I saw things, though. A splash of vodka in her water; a midafternoon visitor on his favourite leather recliner while Joslyn had the tots out for a failed photo op with Jolly Saint Nick.

Becky's tenth Christmas marked a drastic change. Dad was no longer present, off with a new family in South Florida. The stack of gifts, though, had tripled in size. So had Becky's anger.

She no longer took her rage out on Anders. But her avoidance of the boy hurt him more than the abuse. It was clear in his eyes. Through bleary vision, Joslyn was blind to it.

Two new guests sat around the tree five years later. Joey, Becky's newest boyfriend, and Ben, the new "dad." He had stopped by with grocery store roses last year. This Christmas he had earned his own seat. The head of the table, to be precise.

Becky wasn't there for her eighteenth Christmas. Or nineteenth, but was back for the twentieth and twenty-first.

When she was twenty-five and Anders, just legal, the two of them came home, each with a guest. A lover.

I couldn't quite figure the reason for their return. They had no one to answer to. Not with Dad's latest postcard from Georgia, and Mom's letter from rehab tossed on the sofa. But still they came and set up the tree.

Mel was excited, overly happy and festive. She tried too hard, but Anders appreciated it. Loved her more for it. Kurt had been all too happy to place the angel on the tree, making sure to stand close and get a good view down the gaping collar of Mel's holiday sweater.

Becky had only just met the rogue, or so it seemed. But that his attention was centered on Mel, on Anders' girl, made her blood boil with a rage which had been simmering deep down in her heart for decades, now.

Why was she not perfect? Why wasn't she enough? Her parents had replaced her, though they spoke of nothing but her beauty. Her father had left her, then her mother. Becky had tried leaving them, but when no one came looking, she returned, lest she be forgotten entirely. Erased and replaced once more.

For the last few months, Kurt had treasured her.

Lavished her with only the good kind of attention. Until today. Christmas of all days.

Kurt should not have been so careless. Becky's thoughts played and flickered like a horror film on her pretty face. Instead of watching Mel's chest as she bounced around the room, he should have been paying attention to his own date. It was her home, after all.

Her home and everything in it.

The silver letter opener made for a handy weapon. A tool to rid her of her most recent betrayal.

As blood splattered the horrified guests, Anders and Mel, both frozen in shock but not in surprise, I felt a surge of power, satisfaction. Becky was a lifelong project. And such a perfect one, too.

Great Uncle Peter had sent me, a harmless tin elf with a crooked grin, an heirloom from Germany all those years ago. Not as a gift to Garrick to hang on the tree because he wished him and his new family well, but as an attempt to rid his own household of the terror I seemed to bring to their family. I could hardly be blamed for that. The incident in 1942. The horror in '67.

I just watched.

A whispered suggestion or two didn't make me

guilty.

I fixed my eyes on Mel, on her growing belly.

My work with Becky was finished the moment she decided to lift that letter opener to Kurt's jugular. Done with after her arrest.

But babies brought hope for the future, didn't they?

THE CHRISTMAS DANCE

By Bianca Rowena

I'M A FIRM believer in the idea that life is *not* as interesting as fiction. I mean, for the average person like me. I don't have much of a romance-life, but that's because I don't find any of the guys I know interesting. Except for my online friend, dot.con, also known as DC. My sisters don't trust him, because his online name is dot.*con*.

But DC is awesome. I've never met him in real life but he *is* a real person, somewhere out there, just not in my city. Or at least I didn't think so…

My two older sisters are twins: tall, blonde, beautiful and cheerful. I'm short, have dark hair, glasses and I'm not cheerful. Well, I suppose I'm actually quite cheerful, on the inside, but I choose to keep my expression monotone for the sake of having to explain my good mood to others. Why? Because I'm an introvert. Not one of those negative, moody introverts, just someone with her own inner world who finds the outer world distracting and unnecessary.

My mom understands I need time alone, but she thinks it's because I want to go to Harvard. In reality I don't study in my room. I finish my homework at school most of the time. It's easy if you don't have distracting friends to hang out with. At home I daydream and write stories, when I pretend to study. I wish it brought in money for us, because we're kind of poor. Sometimes that makes me feel guilty, because I could probably be out there getting a job and helping Mom pay some bills. But let's face it, introverts don't do well with jobs.

We live above a music store. There are book stores, coffee shops and antique shops all along this street. Renting the office space above the music store is cheaper than renting a real apartment, because you're not technically supposed to use office space to live in.

My room is at the front of the building, facing the street. It used to be someone's lavish office with floor to ceiling windows covering the entire front wall. I keep the blinds closed most of the time because you can see clear into my bedroom from the café across the street.

It was cold in my room when I first found out about the dance. Outside the snow swirled in confused circles, catching updrafts from the cars driving by on the street below. The street was busy with holiday shoppers. Directly outside my window some city workers had installed a huge snowflake onto the streetlamp and now it shined brightly into my room. The fluffy snow and festive lights decorating the stores below made me want to leave my window blinds open, which meant I had to keep my lights off, so no one could see in.

My mom and sisters were trying to set me up again and using the dance to do it. They believe I'll come out of my shell if I fall in love with a handsome, young, extroverted guy whose charm will convert me to the other side, the outgoing side of life. What they don't understand is that introversion is not a choice or something you grow out of or change your mind about. It's an orientation.

The only one who understands this is DC.

This was our messaging conversation from last night.

DC: So just don't go to this dance then, if you don't want to.

Me: I have to.

DC: Why?

Me: They're setting me up with some outgoing, handsome 10/10 guy.

DC: Sounds horrible.

Me: I don't even know what he's like. He could be an extrovert AHHHHHH

DC: Don't you know all the guys in your school?

Me: The dance is not at my school. It's at some Eagle Hall.

DC: Ha ha! Old people :D

Me: It's for the grandkids of old people. So it's cool, okay?

DC: Okay. It does sound cool ;)

Me: Shut up.

DC: It will be an adventure ;)

Me: Not really.

DC: Would it be an adventure if I was going?

I left the cursor blinking for a while, when I saw those words. My sisters' comments about him being a 'con' artist ran through my head. But this was DC. *My* DC.

Me: But you live far away.

DC: Well, there's something I haven't told you.

I could hear my sisters' voices already, speaking in unison the way only twins can, *we told you so!*

Me: Let me guess, you're 45 and you bought a ticket to come find me.

DC: No. lol

Me: Then what's the big secret?

DC: |

The cursor blinked incessantly on the screen as I held my breath for his reply. What could it be? I really didn't think he was a creepy stalker. We had joked about meeting before and he'd always sounded defensive about it.

For a while I thought he must be super awkward looking, or something, to make him seem so self-conscious. Then I wondered if he was in a wheelchair, because in his conversations it always sounded as though his mom had to go with him whenever he drove somewhere.

But I didn't want to joke or guess, I just wanted to wait for him to tell me. Unfortunately, my mom barged into my room before he typed anything more and I quickly let him know.

Me: SIR

SIR is the code word for "Someone In Room." So basically, don't type anything you don't want a parent to see.

We said our goodbyes then and I logged out.

That conversation was yesterday and now we are on the road to this dance, with me trying not to smudge the make-up Vanessa, my sister, put on me while I'm thrown left and right in the van as my Mom drives like a maniac.

"Mom, did you watch a stressful episode of the Bachelor or something?" I ask her. Something is definitely up.

"Quiet, I'm thinking," she replies, her eyes wide like her mind is blank.

She pulls out in front of fast moving traffic like we're rushing to the hospital. I grab the front dash and one of my fake nails goes flying off.

I groan. Vanessa and all her fairy-god-mother aspirations. It was her idea to take me out of my last two classes of school to get my hair done. We didn't have enough money for a nail salon, so she got me press-ons. I rip them all off and put them in my purse. Gross.

My mom swerves into the Donut Shop parking lot. I frown. Is this some alternate route to the Eagle Hall that bypasses traffic and will get us there faster? Do they close the doors exactly at seven, leaving the latecomers dancing outside or something? Seriously, what's the rush? But Mom stops in front of the donut shop and puts the van into park.

"Mom?"

"Why don't you grab us some donuts?" she says, acting weirder than usual.

"Are you serious?" I ask. "I thought we were in a hurry. You didn't even let me check my messages at home." I grind my teeth, remembering how I didn't get a chance to see if DC wrote me back. My phone's broken and I missed library time in last period when I planned to check my messages.

Mom ignores me. She is looking in through the Donut Shop windows like she's left her keys in there and is trying to spot them from the van.

"Okay!" she says, seeming satisfied with her scope of the place. "Go get the donuts."

"What?" I sigh and get out of the van. "What kind?"

"Just go!"

I shut the van door and hurry through the flurry of slow falling snowflakes to the front doors.

The Donut Shop is not busy, because its rival donut shop down the street is WAY cooler and everyone goes there instead.

I notice a boy sitting at a chair looking at me, probably because I'm all dressed up, rushing into a donut shop for emergency donuts.

I wait at the front for a cashier. The cheery Christmas music playing over the speakers lifts my mood. Maybe this dance will be fun after all.

I see my mom through the windows, pointing dramatically at something. I shrug my shoulders at her. She's practically eating the steering wheel in some kind of anticipation. I shake my head at her. She wasn't at all excited about the dance yesterday. Maybe she just really wants this donut.

"Excuse me!" I say loudly. A girl looks out at me from the back area, like I'm totally rude. "Can I please have two donuts, to go?"

She walks over and grabs the money out of my hand, but detours to the back to laugh like hyena with some pimply faced boy, before actually getting my donuts. If she doesn't hurry up my mom will eat the steering wheel before I get the donuts to her. I glare daggers in to the cashier's back, but it does nothing to speed her up.

I'm suddenly hit with this feeling that someone is watching me, other than my mom from outside the windows. I turn around. It's the boy sitting by himself. He looks down when I glance his way, returning his attention to the game he's playing on his phone. I'm reminded of when I was that age. I was a loner, too.

"Hello!" The cashier dangles a paper bag in front of my face.

"Oh." I grab the bag. "Thanks."

The boy gets up as I turn to leave and jogs to the doors, opening one for me.

"Thanks," I say, smiling at him. He's my height, if I minus the heals I'm wearing, and he's got this copper coloured wavy hair and baby blue eyes, with a splash of freckles across his cheeks. He has a warm, sweet scent that makes me want to cuddle up to him and get away from the cold air and snowflakes wafting in. The honking of a car's horn startles me out of my trance. I run to the van.

"So?" My mom asks as I jump in.

"So, what?" I toss the donut bag onto the dash as we pull out of the parking lot.

"What did you think of that boy in the donut shop?" my mom asks, completely disinterested in the donuts I just bought.

"Mom, he's like thirteen or something. I'm six-teen."

"Actually, he'll be turning fifteen in a few days."

My first thought is that DC's birthday is coming up in three days and I need to remember to send a funny e-card. He'll be turning eighteen. I thought it was cool that I was friends with a seventeen-year-old and soon he'll be eighteen. I'm only sixteen, but we get along well. Girls mature faster than boys anyway.

"But you're right," my mom continues. "He looks younger than I thought." She points her finger in the air, letting go of the steering wheel and making me nervous.

"He's too young for anything more than friend-ship," she continues, then talks for a while about how guys are immature. "But anyway," she concludes. "Derek said if you weren't disappointed with your first impres-sions of him to meet him at the Hall."

"He's nice," I shrug, stifling a grin. Could it be that my sisters finally got it right for once? I'm assuming Mom means the boy in the coffee shop. A bit too young for me. He'd be in grade… nine? But I could probably get along with him, for one evening at least.

"You seem unexcited," Mom says. "I thought you said he was your best friend of all time."

"Who?"

I glance at Mom, wondering if her cholesterol pills are making her confuse things again.

"Your internet buddy, Dot.com."

"It's Dot.con, Mom."

My internet buddy…

I jump up, my seatbelt digging into my shoulder. That boy in the donut shop was DC? The same boy who talks with me late into the night and calls me princess sometimes? The same one who understands me better than anyone else in the world?

His real name is Derek? I smile.

So that was his secret, that he was lying about his age.

I look expectantly out the car window as we pull up at the Eagle Hall. A woman is waving at us. We get out of the van and my mom and Derek's mom start chatting it up like only two extroverted moms can.

I have no idea how they know each other, but right now, I don't care. I scurry past them to head for front doors of the emaciated looking Eagle Hall.

"Alanna!" my Mom yells. I stop. "Come say hi to Derek's Mom."

I backtrack, putting on a smile for Derek's mom. She looks nice enough, like a regular mom. But I know she's one of those crazy, overprotective mom's, because I've talked to her son. For a second, I'm worried she'll find me lacking and decide I'm not allowed to be friends with her son anymore.

"Hello," I say to her, trying to remain calm. Am I supposed to shake her hand?

"Nice to finally meet you, Alanna." She's smiling but I can see her assessing me with her eyes. "Derek went inside."

"I'll go find him," I say, eager to leave, eager to see DC and his freckled cheeks and clear blue eyes.

Mom gives me a 'you-be-good' look before I turn to walk away. I want to run, but I can feel the mothers watching me from behind. My heart pounds and I wobble on my heels a bit like I'm drunk.

Once inside, I remove my heels, not trusting my ability to walk at the moment and also not wanting to be taller than DC… Derek.

Then I see him, leaning back against the wall and playing on his phone. I suddenly feel nervous. Why does he have to be so perfect? People who are online all day should be awkward and strange and socially inept.

He looks up and our eyes meet. He almost drops his phone, then catches it at the last second. The floor feels cool beneath my bare feet as I make my way closer. Music pounds noisily from the inner room where the dance has already started. Derek puts his phone away in his pocket.

If we were chatting online right now I'd say 'I can't believe you're here! I can't believe our moms know each other!' But instead, I say nothing at all, because this is real life and talking in real life to someone you like is a lot harder than typing them a message.

Derek smiles. "You look great."

Our eyes meet again and I remember that he isn't shy. He may be introverted but I've known him long enough to know he isn't shy.

He smiles knowingly, his playful grin making my insides swirl. I begin to swing my high heels in my hand, nervously. Derek reaches over and takes them from my hand, setting them down on the floor.

"Would you like to dance, Alanna?" he asks, using my online name. Hearing it brings on a wave of emotion. I start to remember all the history we have together, like the time Timbit, my cat, went missing and DC stayed up chatting with me all night, so I wouldn't be sad.

He closes the gap between us now, taking my hand in his and interlacing our fingers. I'm not used to having anyone close like this. My muscles feel weak, as though my knees might buckle.

DC pulls me closer, setting one hand behind my back in a waltz-style embrace. Just when I think we're about to start dancing and my legs freeze up as I realize I don't know how to waltz, DC leans forward and kisses me…

"Alanna!" My mom's piercing voice breaks the spell. "Will you PUT that notebook away already? You're not skipping school today just to write stories. I thought you said you were sick."

"I am sick," I mumble. I'm sick and tired of being

the only 13-year-old in my class who hasn't been kissed. I'm sick and tired of having no friends. Now, I've got to be honest with you here. I'm not 16 and I've never met DC, although he is my online friend who I've fallen in love with.

But I did make up this story (sorry), well most of it. I mean, we are still poor, and I do have a crazy mom. My life has always been on the page or on the computer screen, in my writing and in my online friendships, not in this dreary world of tangible things, where there is never enough money, and where real-live people are selfish and boring.

This story, however, led to the biggest drama of my life. What *really* happened at the winter dance and all that followed thereafter? That's what I'll be writing next. Sharing this story (and who I shared it with) started a chain of events that forever changed my life, for both good and bad. Because when you finally come out of an introverted cocoon, you enter into this good, bad and ugly thing called 'real life.'

ARE YOU SURE THERE ISN'T A SANTA CLAUS?

By Ken Orich

I CAN'T REMEMBER exactly when I was told there was no Santa Claus. It was probably when I was in grade one or two, or maybe even grade three. I'm pretty sure a classmate is responsible for shattering my Christmas dreams that year. I can vaguely remember him laughing at me and telling me to "grow up" and "get real."

I remember being very confused. I didn't say anything at first because I couldn't. Santa always ate the cookies and drank at least some of the milk we left out for him. Rudolph would always have at least a bite of the carrots we left out for the reindeer!

When I told my older brother Reg there might not be a Santa Claus, he confirmed that he'd learned about that a few years ago, the same way I did. Mom had told him not to spoil it for the rest of us. Now he warned me not to spoil it for our younger brothers. He pointed out we still got Christmas presents anyhow, they just didn't come from Santa. Well, at least I still had the Easter Bunny!

Years went by; Christmases were fun, even if there wasn't a Santa Claus.

I noticed parents were still telling their children about Santa Claus and threatening them with the "naughty" list. Santa was everywhere during the Christmas Season.

We began having children of our own and Santa Claus became a reality again. They were warned about Santa's list and the fact he always checked it twice. My kids always had a tough time making the grade, but they believed. Cookies and milk were put out for Santa on Christmas Eve. Carrots were put out for Rudolph and the rest of the reindeer.

My children wrote letters to Santa at the North Pole and I went with them to deposit those letters in Santa's very own mailbox. It said "Santa Claus, North Pole" on it. He had a mailbox in High Level and one in Slave Lake. I know, I was there. I saw it with my very own eyes. Letters addressed to Santa and put in those mailboxes were answered. Our kids believed!

Santa has been around for a long, long time. Oh, some skeptics will say he is just a myth, but myths are usually based on a truth. The truth just gets changed as it is passed on.

NORAD has tracked Santa's progress from the North Pole on Christmas Eve since 1955. Is it possible that an organization like the North American Aerospace Defense Command could be wrong? They are a government agency established to protect North America. It is unthinkable they would waste their time on such foolishness, if there wasn't a Santa Claus!

The first time I saw the movie "Miracle on 34th Street," something moved me. It was deep inside, just a feeling that has grown with the years. I've watched it every Christmas Season for over forty years now. There seems to be a truth there.

Why does Santa make people smile? Why do we insist on taking our children to the mall Santa and having pictures taken? Why do we continue to tell our children and grandchildren about Santa Claus and his reindeer? Why do our pets get a gift from Santa?

Why do we have our children write letters to Santa? Why do we have them hang up their stockings? Why do we threaten them with the "naughty" list? Why do we smile when we see little kids get all excited about Santa? Why do we do it?

I think because deep down, in our hearts, we believe. Look around and tell me you don't believe.

I do, and that makes it the best Christmas ever.

GRANDMA'S EX-BOYFRIEND

By Sarah Deverall

"GRANDMA GOT RUN *over by a reindeer, Walking home from our house Christmas Eve...*"

I punched the radio dial to turn that horrible song off. I despised that song with a passion... almost as much as I despise the hustle and bustle of Christmas shopping. I never used to be a Grinch. But what happened the Christmas of 1982 when I was a lad of eleven and too big to believe in Santa Claus and his nine not-so-tiny reindeer, changed that. Let me tell you my tale of woe.

I was excited that Grandma Johnson was coming to our house for Christmas. Since Grandpa George passed away that spring, we didn't want her to be alone. She took the bus from the neighbouring town of Donnerville and Dad picked her up from the depot. On the way home, he stopped to get our traditional Christmas Eve dinner of fried chicken, fries, gravy and coleslaw.

We usually have it delivered as Dad liked to play Cupid for my older sister, Jenny. At twenty-one, I think they believed she would never leave unless they found her a nice boy with a job and his own car.

We rushed out the front door to meet Grandma with hugs and kisses. Grandma was a feisty old broad, with a poof of lavender grey hair permed in a cloud about her head. That night, she was wearing a lime green velour dress and glittery red sneakers. If it weren't for her sweet wrinkly face, she would fit in with the girls at my brother William's high school. Even my buddy Rob's grandpa said she was a vixen, out to break the hearts of the men at the Donnerville Senior Center.

But this week was all about cheering up Grandma and maybe we'd see her Blitzen smile again.

After supper, Grandma said she felt hot and the house was too stuffy (Dad did like to have a roaring fire in the fireplace). Grandma decided to take a stroll around the block. We warned her about the icy sidewalks and the tough kids down the street that might dash her into the wall and steal her purse. She countered that she would leave her purse behind and off she went.

I had already changed into my pajamas and brushed my teeth when I heard the sirens. My face lit up with glee at seeing an accident on our street.

My siblings and I ran outside in our PJs and slippers, ignoring Mom's shouts to put on our coats and boots. We pushed past the adults to get close to the flashing lights. It was a most horrifying sight.

There on the ground was Grandma, skirt up to her waist, and her red glittery sneakers wrapped around Santa's waist as she pummeled him with her fists.

"Mommy! Dat lady's hurting Santa!" a child cried out.

"Ma'am! Ma'am! Let Mr. Claus go," said Officer Wilson who lived three doors down from us.

Grandma sat up and karate chopped Santa's jugular, and pulled his beard.

"This old fool should have had his license revoked years ago. He's a menace to society. Did you see what he did?" She glared at the police officer and rubbed her arm. "He deliberately ran those beasts into me."

She pointed to the nine reindeer grazing on the dried crab-apples littering the boulevard. Someone had cut the leather leads, which had bound them to the sleigh.

The old fashioned sled lay tipped on its side. The large red velvet sack had spilling its contents of brightly wrapped packages onto the ice covered street.

"Do we have a witness to this alleged accident?" Officer Wilson pulled out his notebook and scanned the crowd. Most people were dressed in their festive holiday pajamas, festooned with holly, Christmas trees, snowmen, or Rudolph the Red-Nosed Reindeer. A few others were more elegantly attired in suits and ties; Mrs. Peters was in a full out Cinderella ball gown.

"I did, Officer Wilson." A small hand was raised as Suzie pushed past the adults, pulling her baby brother, Tommy behind her. "We were on Santa Watch." She raised the binoculars that dangled from her neck and pointed to another similarly attired child across the street. "James saw it too."

Officer Wilson knelt down beside the little girl. "What did you see, Suzie?"

"Well, Grandma Johnson was walking down the sidewalk, pushing her walker. We saw Santa's reindeer come flying down from the sky. The sleigh hit the street and sparks flew from the runners. Rudolph and the other reindeer couldn't get traction on the ice and they sideswiped Billy's van." She pointed to the van down the street, it's Barbarian Babe riding a White Tiger graphic scraped and dented.

"Dude! My van!" A pimply faced teenager cried and raced toward his prized possession.

"Anyway," James took up the tale. "Rudolph tried to stop." He giggled. "His nose was blinking a distress signal and he was making and 'Ee-Aw' sound like a siren. Grandma Johnson was trying to get away but she slipped on a patch of ice on the Tribbet's driveway and fell. She got hit by one of the deer's hooves."

Officer Wilson espied the discarded walker at the end of the Tribbet's driveway. He held back a grin. *Wait until the guys at the precinct hear this story.* He walked over to where Santa was sprawled on the ground. Someone had pulled Grandma off him and he was slowly coming around.

"Excuse me, Mr. Claus, sir." Officer Wilson squatted next to the legend. "Could you tell me what happened. How did you lose control of your sleigh?"

Santa sat up, clutching his head and hiccupped.

Wilson frowned, leaning in to take a sniff of the old man. "Mr. Claus, have you been drinking?"

A gasp erupted from the assembled crowd. *Santa was drunk? Would he be arrested for drunk driving?*

Santa shook his head, groaned and sighed. "Only a nip or two. It helps me digest all the milk and cookies the children leave out for me." He raised pleading eyes to Officer Wilson. "Oh, please don't tell Harriet. She'll skin me alive. That woman has quite a temper." He looked abashed. "I was heading to a 7-11." He pointed to the neon sign visible two blocks away. "I was hoping a six-pack of that new Green Comet energy drink would help me get through the night."

"Help me up, Son." Santa grabbed the hand of the young man in a green suit. "Thank you, Gordon. Glad to see you finally got the nerve up to ask Katherine out." He waved to the blushing girl in a short orange dress. "You two will be very happy together."

Officer Wilson nodded as his partner stepped forward with a small device. "I'm sorry to do this, Mr. Claus, but could you blow into the Breathalyzer, please." He held the device to Santa's mouth. "Now blow with all your might."

Santa huffed and exhaled into the mouthpiece. His stubby fingers moved to the digital reader.

"Uh uh, Santa." Officer Wilson retrieved the Breathalyzer. "No resetting the device." He looked down at the small screen. "1.2," he frowned, disappointment in his expression. He gripped Santa's arm and pulled the fat man forward. "I'm sorry, Sir, but you are over the legal limit and you are under arrest for impaired driving."

More gasps of shock and exclamations of displeasure echoed through the crowd.

"No!"

"You can't."

"It would ruin Christmas."

"I realize that this is a travesty." Officer Wilson leaned against the police cruiser. "But I took an oath to uphold the law and keep drunk drivers off our streets," he gazed up at the heavens, "and the sky."

"But what about all the toys he still has to deliver?" Several people cried from where they were packing parcels back into Santa's bag. "Who will deliver them?"

"I will." Grandma stood as tall as her 5'2" frame could, hand on her hips. "I will be Nick's designated driver."

I looked over at my brother and sister in shock as

I mouthed the word, "Nick." *Grandma was on a first name basis with Santa?*

"Alright, Mrs. Johnson. I am handing Mr. Claus into your custody, but he must return to Northtown Police Station first thing tomorrow morning."

Officer Wilson was interrupted by his partner. "Ah, Sir? That would be Christmas morning, Sir."

"I realize that Cameron," Officer Wilson sighed. "Alright, Santa is to be at the Precinct on December 26th at 9am to be formally charged with impaired driving causing bodily harm and property damage." He nodded his head toward Billy who was still crying over the damages done to his van.

"Constable Cameron will be your guard," Wilson snickered. "Elf for the night. He will ensure your compliance and return."

The young constable grinned, his face alight with excitement.

"Alright, people. Let's get this sleigh upright and hitched up. Ladies, if you would be so kind as to finish gathering the parcels back into the sack." In short order, the sleigh was loaded and the reindeer hitched using strands of Christmas lights in lieu of the cut leather straps.

Grandma took up the reins while Santa sat back against the seat, moaning about how Harriet would not be pleased when she saw him with his old girlfriend.

My mouth fell open. *Grandma was Santa's ex-girlfriend?*

"Okay, Nick," Grandma's voice was stern. "How do I get this thing to go?"

"On Dasher, on Dancer, on Prancer and Vixen. On Comet and Cupid and Donner and Blitzen…"

So that boys and girls is my story about how Grandma almost ruined Christmas. Not that it was her fault by any means. Who knew Santa had a drinking problem? Brought on by lost love and a duty that led him to marry another woman, perhaps?

Just think, if all had gone as Grandma had hoped as a young lady, I might have been Santa's grandkid!

GETTING READY FOR CHRISTMAS

By Leslie Johnson

SANDRA PULLED THE lid off the plastic tote filled with Christmas decorations. She sat down on the coffee table and let her emotions swirl over her. How was she ever going to get ready for the big day when her heart was still in tiny pieces? After several minutes, she let out a long sigh and pushed herself to her feet.

With the practiced precision of someone who'd decorated over forty-five trees in her adult lifetime, she clipped two strings of lights to the boughs of the real evergreen tree that had been delivered and set up by her son earlier that day.

Hours went by and she only stared at the tree, sitting in it's usual spot in the living room. She waited to hear her husband, Doug, come home, stomping off snow from his boots and calling for her to put on the coffee. But he never came home. Not because he didn't want to, she supposed. But because he was buried six feet deep in Hillcrest Cemetery across town.

Grabbing a couple of glass baubles from the tote, she began draping them on the tips of the tree branches. She stepped back occasionally to eye the tree, looking for a gap in the placement or a clump of them hanging too close to one another.

The last decorations that went up were the ones her son had made in grade school. They were time-worn and precious. These always got prime placement – a reflection of their importance.

At the bottom of the tote were a few holly branches and other greenery for the hearth and the banisters. When she pulled out the first length of garland she saw it. Just the corner at first. It was there, under the mistletoe.

She shifted everything aside and retrieved the picture. It was an old Polaroid instant snap taken forty-five years before. Tears welled up blurring the image. She wiped them away absently as her arms and legs began to tremble. Over-whelming love spread throughout, seeping into the cracks of her broken heart.

Feeling unsettled and weak, Sandra left the decorating behind and walked into the kitchen. She sat heavily at the table. At first, she sat there quietly, holding the picture in front of her – staring at the image of their first Christmas - her and Doug's. They were so young, so full of life and love. Where had the time gone? Her mind raced through a multitude of moments, each one lifting away a little of the scab that had hardened over her heart the day Doug died.

She lay the picture carefully on the table in front of her, closed her eyes and wept. For the first time since she left the hospital that last day – tears washed down her cheeks and dripped off her chin. She heard Doug's booming laugh, his gentle words, his concern, his love.

Her heart, swollen with unshed sorrow, burst open and more tears poured out until Sandra felt she couldn't take another minute. Still, the images came, wrapping themselves around her, cuddling her and then releasing her to the next. The bad memories, the ones that she'd been living with for months, those last dark days of

Doug's illness and hospitalization were banished, replaced by moments that brought a sparkle back to Sandra's eyes.

Visions from the past burst into her mind, one after another. The look on Doug's face as he stared at his newborn son; Doug presenting her with tickets to a sold out concert she'd wanted to see; taking Doug a cup of coffee as he worked on his old cars in the garage, sitting on the high stool watching him tinker; working in their vegetable garden together. Doug's pride in his tomatoes; the road trip they took to the Yukon one summer when the kids were young; the yearly trip to Waterton Lakes and the annual family photo in front of Cameron Falls.

Every memory built on the last, a lifetime of love and togetherness, filling Sandra with emotions that she had thought she'd never feel again. The experience sucked the life out of her bones and then poured it back in, refreshed. She lived her life again, only this time she saw it with the value it deserved. Those precious moments taken for granted were cherished and embraced for the gift they were.

It took hours. Long after the sun had gone down, long after the street outside had gone to bed, she sat there in the dark, remembering.

Finally, the memories exhausted, she longed for bed. Passing by the living room, she caught sight of the tree in the window. Standing next to it, in silhouette, was Doug. She blinked, unable to believe what she was seeing. The image shifted as it came toward her. She felt no fear - only a wave of love.

She moved toward her husband, his features taking form. He stopped and held something up over his head. She recognized it. The mistletoe. She stepped into his arms and his lips found hers. Home at last.

"Where have you been?" she whispered as they pulled apart.

"Right here," Doug replied, pointing at her heart. "Where I've always been and where I'll stay until you come to me."

"I want to come now. I can't live without you."

"It's not time. You've got some love to spend on those grandsons of ours. They need you."

"I know they do. But I need *you*."

"And I'm right here – always."

Contented, she closed her eyes and nestled against his chest. His arms tightened around her. She sighed.

Waking hours later, she was in bed alone. Panicked, she climbed out of bed and hurried down the hall to the living room. The tree stood against the window, only this time there was no silhouette. Her heart fell and she sank onto the couch.

"I'm right here," she heard Doug say as she felt something touch her heart. Placing her right hand there, she felt his fingers under hers. With a sigh, she felt peace settle inside.

Plugging in the lights on the tree – Sandra knew that she was finally ready for Christmas. "Thank you, my love," she whispered. "Until we meet again."

Acknowledgements

The River Bottom Writers would like to give special thanks to Bianca Rowena, for publishing their first anthology, *Silt,* and to Leslie Johnson, for faithfully leading the group for over six years.

Thank you to all the members who have attended over the years, especially those still meeting weekly and keeping our group vibrant and strong.

A heartfelt thanks to all of our family and friends, who have supported us along the way, and our fellow writing colleagues from across Southern Alberta.

A very special thanks to Sandy Charlton, for offering his time to edit stories to our members for this anthology. And last, but certainly not least, a big thank you to the readers and those who support local authors and writers in our community.

About the Authors

Leslie Johnson is the founder of the River Bottom Writers in Lethbridge, Alberta. Growing up on a ranch in Waterton, Leslie enjoyed swimming in the river, riding horses and writing works inspired by the beautiful Canadian landscapes around her. Leslie writes literary fiction with strong women protagonists.

A long-time resident of Lethbridge, ***Bryan L. Beerling*** has been writing since his school days and has been a professional journalist, a father, husband and grandfather. These life experiences, especially time spent with his two grandchildren, have given Bryan the inspiration to write his stories. When asked what genre of writing he prefers he simply answers "LIFE."

Actively seeking publication of her novels, ***Amanda Chomiak*** is a romance writer who loves creating happily ever afters for her characters almost as much as she adores her Welsh Terrier, Gromit. A member of the River Bottom Writers for six years, Amanda holds her BA and MA in History from the U of L and studied with Winghill Writing School.

Sarah Deverall grew up with an active imagination that became a passion for writing. Her genre of choice is Romance both contemporary and historical, but she also dabbles in fantasy and children's fiction. She lives in Lethbridge, AB with her three cats, works at the local hospital and likes to garden and travel in her free time.

Megan Fennell enjoys drinking coffee and making things up, typically about monsters, mad scientists, and shady corporations. She is one half of the Lethbridge writing duo, V. F. LeSann, and her short stories have been published through the likes of On Spec Magazine, Edge Publishing, World Weaver Press, and more.

Charles James (Charles Kirkby) is a dad, husband, medical physicist, an adjunct associate professor at the University of Calgary and has been a member of Lethbridge's River Bottom Writers since 2015.

Ken Orich is an avid birder and photographer. Retired after 35 years as a Wildfire Specialist, Ken writes about his life experiences and observations made in nature. He enjoys growing hot peppers and making salsa and is the writer for the 'Bird of the Week' articles on the Helen Schuler Nature Centre Facebook Page.

Vanessa Rieswyk has been a faithful member of the River Bottom Writers for four years. She loves animals, especially dogs, as well as reading, writing and making new friends. Vanessa's stories and poems reflect her lively imagination and unique view of the world around her.

Bianca Rowena is the author of *The Virgin Diaries,* as well as the Young Adult novels *The Gift Stone* and *Takano Rynn.* She lives in Southern Alberta with her husband and daughter. For more information about Bianca, visit: www.biancarowena.com

Brock Sansome has been published in other Anthologies, including the *In Places Between 2014 Edition* Anthology, as a winner in the *When Words Collide* competition for Best Short Fiction. He enjoys writing Fantasy and what can only be described as 'strange' fiction.

Nurse by night, nurse by day and writer somewhere between, ***Shannon Still's*** love of reading and writing were inspired by her mother, aunt, and best friend, Jo. She enjoys all things fantasy, romance, and YA, and hopes to one day see her pseudonym LK Winters on a published book of her own.

Randy Ward is the author of the popular novel *You Can't Make This S#it Up!* A retired police officer of 27 years, he's been involved in many aspects of policing, including Street Patrol, Break and Enter detail and the Criminal Investigation Division.

Randy has been married for over 40 years and is the father of three boys, as well as a grandfather.

Tom Yeoman has been a member of the River Bottom Writers for over six years.

A Lethbridge-based commentator and videographer, Tom enjoys reading and writing science fiction.

95948746R10184

Made in the USA
Middletown, DE
28 October 2018